Dashiell Hammett's

AGAINST THE BAR

IT'S ALL PRETTY

Selected Stories from the 2018
Literary Taxidermy Short Story Competition

Edited by

MARK MALAMUD

AGAINST THE BAR

First Regulus Press printing November 2018
Signal Library 20-8102-71-01

Regulus Press, Seattle WA
www.regulus.press

ISBN: 0999446232
ISBN-13: 978-0999446232
(Regulus Press)

OPPORTUNITIES FOR
FUTURE TAXIDERMY

"This is my favorite book in all the world, although I have never read it. It's just fairer than death, that's all."
— WILLIAM GOLDMAN, *THE PRINCESS BRIDE*

"You will rejoice to hear that no disaster has accompanied the commencement of an enterprise which you have regarded with such evil forebodings. He was soon borne away by the waves and lost in darkness and distance."
— MARY SHELLEY, *FRANKENSTEIN*

"I was out with Blood, my dog. A boy loves his dog."
— HARLAN ELLISON, "A BOY AND HIS DOG"

"All children, except one, grow up. When Margaret grows up she will have a daughter, who is to be Peter's mother in turn; and thus it will go on, so long as children are gay and innocent and heartless."
— J.M. BARRIE, *PETER PAN*

"On an exceptionally hot evening early in July a young man came out of the garret in which he lodged in S. Place and walked slowly, as though in hesitation, towards K. bridge. That might be the subject of a new story, but our present story is ended."
— F. DOSTOYEVSKY, *CRIME AND PUNISHMENT*

"This is written from memory, unfortunately. With which agreement we at last left Herland."
— CHARLOTTE PERKINS GILMAN, *HERLAND*

"We went to the Moon to have fun, but the Moon turned out to completely suck. Everything must go."
— M. T. ANDERSON, *FEED*

"On our wedding day I was forty-six, she was eighteen. And we rode forward into the night, past the sleeping houses of our countrymen."
— GEORGE SANDERS, *LINCOLN IN THE BARDO*

"David Bowie took one last sip of water then tossed the empty paper cup into the trash. 'Seventy-two raisins, you mean,' said God — and they both had a good laugh as Disco raced for his guns."
— MARK MALAMUD, *FLOAT THE POOCH*

"I have never begun a novel with more misgiving. And however superciliously the highbrows carp, we the public in our heart of hearts all like a success story; so perhaps my ending is not so unsatisfactory after all."
— W. S. MAUGHAM, *THE RAZOR'S EDGE*

I was leaning against the bar in a speakeasy on 52nd street, waiting for Nora to finish her Christmas shopping, when a girl got up from the table where she had been sitting with three other people and came over to me.

↓

"That may be," Nora said, "but it's all pretty unsatisfactory."

— Dashiell Hammett, first and last line from *The Thin Man*

CONTENTS

Introduction

Welcome to *Against the Bar*, one of three anthologies that collect the prize-winning stories from the 2018 Literary Taxidermy Short Story Competition.

Literary taxidermy is a story-writing process that involves taking the first and last sentence from a well-known work (often a novel, but sometimes a short story) and then "re-stuffing" what goes in-between those lines to create a new, wholly-original narrative. The goal of the literary taxidermist is not just to slap someone else's words onto the start and finish of an otherwise stand-alone story, but to take full ownership of the borrowed lines, interpreting (or re-interpreting) them in order to make them seamless, integral, and in fact the *perfect* start and finish for the new story being told.

The origin of literary taxidermy is *The Gymnasium*, a collection of nineteen stories written between 2003 and 2017 that "re-stuff" classic works by Milan Kundera, Thomas Wolfe, Ian Fleming, and others. The earliest stories started as little more than a casual prompted-writing exercise, a quick & dirty way to keep my hands busy between other, larger projects. The twist of providing both a start and finish as part of the prompt wasn't deeply considered. I am a believer in creative parsimony, also known as laziness, and so the idea of leveraging the words of another writer in this way seemed both simple and convenient. There was a certain novelty, to be sure; but there's novelty in throwing open cans of paint against a canvas, too. It might seem like a good idea at the time — it might in fact *be* a good idea at the time — who doesn't enjoy a moment of chaotic release? — but that doesn't mean you end up with anything worthwhile.

But I got lucky.

It turned out there was something surprisingly satisfying about working within this particular delimited structure, balancing appropriation and originality, managing another's voice and my own, and charting a new path to a known destination. Very quickly those "other, larger projects" fell aside. My quick & dirty exercise had become a full-time obsession. Many stories followed.

During those early days, my curiosity was focused on where each pair of first and last lines (some of them with quite well-known trajectories) would take *me*; but that changed when — about halfway through what would become *The Gymnasium* — I enjoined several other writers to co-participate in my literary experiment. We'd each take the same first/last lines, go off for a week or two, then return to compare our efforts. The results — "sibling stories" we called them — made me realize that there was another collection I wanted to see: a book composed entirely of stories that all start and end the same way, but written by different authors.

Which brings us to the anthology you hold in your hands and the competition that produced it.

The Literary Taxidermy Short Story Competition, sponsored by Regulus Press, invites writers to stitch together their own stories using the opening and closing sentences of classic works of fiction. For the 2018 competition, aspiring writers were given three choices: *The Thin Man* by Dashiell Hammett; *Through the Looking-Glass* by Lewis Carroll; or "A Telephone Call" by Dorothy Parker.

The present anthology contains stories from the Hammett contest. That means that every story you're about to read starts and ends *exactly* the same way — with the first and last sentence of the novel *The Thin Man* by Dashiell Hammett. Of course *the path* that each author takes from beginning to end is unique — and therein lies a particular thrill of reading these short works: despite sharing a common frame, they are all *different*.

So some of the stories in this collection are sharp, some are sad, some are erotic, some are broad farce, and some are just *strange*. They cross genres; they cross continents (and occasionally planets); and they vary in style and diction and tone and voice. Reading each one is like getting a peek at the results of someone else's Rorschach test.

The authors are eclectic, too. They range in age from twenty-one to seventy-five. They also span the globe, so you're about to read stories from the United States, Canada, Taiwan, India, New Zealand, Colombia, and the UK. (And that's why you may notice stories written in British and American English — so don't be shocked to find *colour* in one story and *color* in the next.) The winning author in this year's Hammett contest is Shanta Gyanchand, a British writer living in Pune, India. Her story "Genesis" is a futuristic tale of uncertainty, memory, and change.

But there's more to these stories than the pleasure found in their distinction or their differences. Their *similarities* can be just as intriguing.

Yes, you will find a number of stories within this collection that are about mobsters and booze — after all, the opening line is *I was leaning against the bar in a speakeasy on 52nd street, waiting for Nora to finish her Christmas shopping, when a girl got up from the table where she had been sitting with three other people and came over to me.*

And the last line — *"That may be," Nora said, "but it's all pretty unsatisfactory."* — guarantees there are numerous tales that turn on disappointment.

But *those* similarities are not especially interesting. What's interesting are the similarities that appear in story after story that are *unexpected*. For example, this contest received a statistically-improbable number of stories that include questions of memory, the afterlife, and homburg hats. Why? What is it about *those* two lines by Dashiell Hammett that trigger *these* particular narrative neurons to fire?

Literary taxidermy is nothing if not a kind of inkblot test, an invitation to interpret and then riff inside an ambiguous narrative frame. Even if the bizarre similarities that emerge are inexplicable (and really: why *do* so many of the Hammett stories have girls named after flowers?), it shouldn't be a shock that the same input yields similar output. And yet the black box in-between — the human imagination — remains a mystery.

I really had no idea what to expect when Regulus Press launched this competition, but in the end I was amazed and inspired by the enthusiasm of the response. The stories in all three anthologies (this one, as well as *Telephone Me Now* and *One Thing Was Certain* for the Parker and Carroll contests) were selected anonymously by myself, the editors at Regulus Press, and a panel of eight professional-writer judges. The stories are entertaining, intriguing, and occasionally shocking. After each story, you'll find a short biographical note about the author, and maybe — just maybe — *you* can figure out how they ended up writing the story they did!

Mark Malamud
3 October 2018

Stories between the Floors

I WAS LEANING against the bar in a speakeasy on 52nd street, waiting for Nora to finish her Christmas shopping, when a girl got up from the table where she had been sitting with three other people and came over to me.

"I know you," she said. It was impossible to tell if she did. Upgrades and aesth implants had made a mess of her tells. Goddamned planet-bound neosynths. Too many resources and too little responsibility. Her friends at the table looked about the same.

"Do you, now?" I asked her. There wasn't much else to ask. No point in denying what I had no way of knowing the truth of.

"Yeah," she told me, "you're that station-born gal who shacked up with the cloistered gal from behind the Urea paywall, right? You live down on 32nd, between 'facturing floors?"

"Uriel. It's some kind of angel," I corrected. I tried to flag the bartender down for another drink, but the damned robot ignored me. That was the problem with isolating them from the Network: their A.I. got all screwy after a while. "What of it?"

"No need to get so frosty, doll," she said, running her fingers over the soundports above her collarbones like my words had made them itch. "I was just curious. I heard about you, wanted to say hello."

"Curious ain't a good thing to be, given the law and where we're standing," I told her. "Now you've said hello.

I'm sure your friends must be missing you." Judging by the number of cables her friends had started plugging into each other, they didn't look like they were, but that was none of my business. I tapped the bar again. Still no luck.

"Aw, come on, doll," she pouted, if that's something you could call that particular expression on lips that were half aesth and no hint of skin. "Tell me a story. I've never been off-world."

Oh, trust me, darling, *I know*, I wanted to tell her. The planet-bound came in two colours: hers and the hardworking people who wanted out but couldn't afford it. For the same reason a cat doesn't leave a sunbeam to sit under a bunklight, her kind never left planetside. Real chrome types. Shiny and useless.

"You want stories, you get that goddamned barkeep out of its protocol loop so I can get another drink," I said. She laughed. It was just about the most human thing I ever saw her do.

"You got it, doll," she said, and plugged something into somewhere, hands going between her waist and the port banks under the bar. I didn't look long. I never do. It makes me nauseous.

Goddamn the thing, but it did come when she called it like that, whirring and clicking like no well-maintained service robot ever does. I remember thinking it had the sort of face that was popular in bars on higher levels, closer to the agri-leisure floors, and the kind of hands that had stopped being popular years ago. A real mix job, the kind you only ever saw on the lower levels, where drink wasn't allowed. Gave the workers problems, they said. Have a drink upstairs, on your next vacation, they said. Real old-world addict rhetoric bullshit. People kept drinking. Sometimes people went blind. See, just like we told you, they said. Nobody reads the history books and nothing ever changes.

"Gin? Isn't that old-fashioned of you. I would've

thought you liked station-style brewers," she told me. I must've looked just the same as I felt right then, because she followed it with, "Oh, honey, just because this place is off-Network doesn't mean it doesn't track what you're drinking. I've got your tab, so be sweet a minute with me, doll: about that story?"

They always wanted to hear the same things: yes, ma'am, it's a hard life stationside. No, ma'am, I never saw a real tree before I hit dirt here. Yes, ma'am, my bones are kind of funny, gravity comps tend to fritz and when you spend most of your middle years in low-grav it does funny things to a person's body. No, ma'am, I ain't leaning 'cause my bones are funny, I'm leaning 'cause a body likes to lean sometimes.

Laughing, she was almost pretty. *Almost.* Looking at her as a woman, I'd need more than 'dustrial batch gin to get past the sculptures she'd built under her skin, but I could say she was pretty like something that ought to have been in a museum, at least.

"And how'd you meet your Urea girl?" she asked me.

I didn't correct her a second time. If she hadn't learned the first, she wasn't going to. "Folks born behind the paywall grow up not knowing there's anything outside their floor," I said. "How she tells it, life out here might as well have ended for how little her parents talked about their lives before they passed the paywall and started living amongst the congregation. She said her daddy was missing an eye-big chunk of his head just gone where they took out his upgrades."

I don't much care for scaring people, but I will admit I took a certain satisfaction in how clear her fear was when she touched the landscape she'd made of her own face.

"Anyway, she was a curious type, like you," I said, knowing full well this was a lie. My Nora was as different from this creature in front of me as humans could be from one another, but it got me what I wanted: another gin. "She liked to poke around the vents in the stopwalls and listen by the old stairwells. One day I guess she managed to get into one or the other — she's not too specific on how she got to another floor. I met her by chance, about a year later, while I was processing low-grav assembly orders stationside. When her face came through on the comm, I thought she was the prettiest thing I'd ever seen."

Even now I couldn't tell you what this girl thought about that. Her face did something, but just what that something was is a question I don't think I'll ever know the answer to.

"Well, I heard it was you who broke her out," she said. It might've been a complaint. I guess she'd expected something a little more exciting.

I shrugged. "Stories get out of hand. You take a pretty woman out from behind a paywall and a moon-legged gal off a station and put'em together? Of course people talk. There's nothing to do down here but talk and drink."

I looked over. Her friends were a mess of cables. I couldn't tell one from the other. I was sure I'd seen three of them at her table when she'd walked over, but there was no way of knowing now.

"Where is your Urea gal?" she asked me, and I started to wonder if she was doing it on purpose. Maybe I'd offended her. There was no way to know, and besides, she'd still paid for all my drinks.

"Christmas shopping," I said. I saw no point in hiding it.

It might've been surprise, that look on her face. "You celebrate?"

"*She* does," I answered truthfully. "Folks don't leave everything behind the paywall."

She started to say something, but I'm not sure what it was. Nora's voice always cuts through: "And how much of our rent money have you poured down your throat while I wasn't around to watch you, Koleena Parkheld?"

I turned. I must've been smiling like a real fool, because she just shook her head. "Next to nothing, sweet thing, my new friend here —" I was polite, I did try to make their introduction, good idea or bad one, but she was just gone. I guess she finally got bored and wandered off, but where to I couldn't tell you. My eyes were filled with Nora, and she was all I saw.

She shook her head again and it was just like the first time. Even when she was frowning, her dark eyes just bewitched me. "Well, if she wants to spend her coin on a big-headed drunkard of a starchild like you, I won't tell her not to, but I'm ready to be on my way."

"As am I, as am I," I told her, gathering my cane and coat, and she slipped her hand into the crook of my arm. "How was shopping? You find everything you wanted to find, sweetness?" As we walked out of the speakeasy, I found that the lights of the roof above us were dimmed for the evening. I hadn't realized how late it had gotten.

"I got as much for as little as I'd dared to hope I might," she said, smiling a little. Goddamn but she was beautiful. "Now we'll have to see if this is the year they'll give consent to meet me between levels so I can give them over."

"This year for sure," I told her, squeezing her hand where it lay in my arm. "They've been softening up, sweet thing, I keep telling you — last year they even threatened us." Our feet and my cane on the concrete of the sidewalk always created a musical sort of patter. The differences in the lengths of our legs meant we never quite fell into step: she had had two strides to my one, with my cane keeping time like a metronome.

"Well, I guess it's better than pretending I don't exist," she sighed. "I still have gifts from five years ago waiting to go over."

"And they will, one day," I said. "We've got time."

"That may be," Nora said, "but it's all pretty unsatisfactory."

"Stories between the Floors"

KALE BROWN was born in a small town named after a fish. These days, when they're not writing about the future, they're a jewelry clerk in the Canadian capital of Ottawa — a large city named after a river. We think that's a step up. "Stories between the Floors" is their first published story, unless you count the single-copy imprint from the secret publishing house in the basement of their elementary school when they were nine.

They say: "I wrote this story in one sitting, without an outline or even a concrete concept of where it was going. I just sat there and felt out the shape of it as I went, letting it grow organically. It was hard to stop writing. I wanted to keep going forever."

Mary Madeleine's Initial Complaint

I WAS LEANING against the bar in a speakeasy on 52nd street, waiting for Nora to finish her Christmas shopping, when a girl got up from the table where she had been sitting with three other people and came over to me.

"I remember you," she said. "You helped me, once."

I looked her up and down and said, "I think you got the wrong lady."

She shook her head. "It was you," she told me. "I was younger then."

I finished my whiskey and said, "Mary Madeleine?"

She curtsied.

"Well, it's good to see you living a good life." I looked over at her table, where her friends watched us very carefully. "*Is it* a good life?"

"They're nervous," she said, waving her hand. "They think you're dangerous, because I spent the last five minutes telling them how you —"

"All right," I said.

"Oh, they don't think you're dangerous now," she said, "but they worry I'm going to get hurt with what I'm asking you to do."

I glanced out the window. I saw Nora cross the street, one neatly wrapped parcel tucked under each arm. This was my plan for the next week: share Christmas with my girl, eat a turkey, and visit my parents, the last one conditional on whether one of the parcels under Nora's arm was a large bottle of gin. Whatever Mary Madeleine was about to say, it was the kind of thing that led to a turkey getting overcooked, and I'd saved for the damn thing for weeks.

"It's about a boy," she said, and I sighed.

When Mary Madeleine came out of her hotel lift into the lobby where we waited, she cocked her head.

"Why are you wearing a wig?"

"I don't know what you mean," I said.

Nora leaned across and whispered, "She's banned from the Barbizon."

Mary Madeleine gasped. "Did you bring a man here? I heard some girls hide boys in the rubbish chute or disguise them as women."

"She *was* the illicit visitor," Nora said.

"Well," Mary Madeleine said, "my parents can't expect to bring me up knowing people like you and then get terribly affronted when I go out on six dates a week."

"Six!" Nora said. "I miss these days," she added wistfully.

"People like *me*?" I asked.

We went into the hotel restaurant and were seated by the window. Mary Madeleine ordered a slice of cheesecake with three forks, and Nora asked for a black coffee and a vanilla milkshake. The waiter smiled at me and said to Nora, "You ever see that Lilian again, you tell her she owes me a dollar. I nearly broke my back carrying her that time."

"Oh, I haven't seen her in years," Nora said. "But if I do, I'll be sure to let her know."

"Broke his back!" I hissed when he left. "*He* was the one who let slip I was hiding behind the door. It's not my fault I had to pretend to be unconscious so he could carry me outside without being caught."

"Don't listen to her perpetual sulking," Nora told Mary

Madeleine. "Honey, what is your problem, and what would you like us to do about him?"

"Well," she said, "I have a job, you see. I'm in advertising."

"I thought you wanted to be a vet?" I said.

"A vet and the first woman to the North Pole," Mary Madeleine said. "But it turns out I'm allergic to cats and women already made it to the North Pole, so now I draw advertising pictures for magazines. You know Leary's Lip Stain?"

"Oh!" Nora said. "*Luminous lips save ships*, yes?"

"I drew that," Mary Madeleine said. "And a version of myself for Curly Candy's Black Hair Pomade. I'll tell you for nothing, I loved these kinks every day until the one where I had to draw them."

"You're doing very well for yourself," I said. "Your daddy must be proud."

"Well, yes," she said, "Except he doesn't believe me. He's suspicious about where I'm really earning my money. He has it in his damn head that I've been doing modelling." She dropped her voice. "Without *clothes* on."

"And what on God's green earth is the problem with that?" Nora said hotly.

I put my hand on hers. "It's a problem if her father thinks something untrue," I said. "They're good people, Nora. Save your wrath for something else."

Mary Madeleine blinked at us both and I remembered for a moment how very young she had been when I set her neighbour on fire. It wasn't very hard to do — he lit the match himself, after all, trying to light up their fence for the third time, unaware he was standing in a puddle of gasoline I had left there for him. I had not factored his piercing screams waking her up to watch it all from her bedroom window.

"Why doesn't he believe you're in advertising?" Nora

asked her.

"I'll show you," she said. "In all the pictures, we leave a tiny signature, yes?" She reached into her bag and brought out a folder; inside was the original picture she had drawn for Leary's Lip Stain. Mary Madeleine tapped a fingernail on one of the ship's boilers. "See, in the shading? M-MK. Mary Madeleine Kennedy." She unfolded a newspaper page. "And this is the finished ad," she said.

Instead of the M-MK, there was a crowded LOUC.

"Louis Callaghan," she said. "He delivers to the printer. He has been replacing my name with his."

Nora hissed, "I will set his entire house on fire."

I put my hand over hers again. "Have you tried talking to your boss?"

"My boss?" she said. "You mean, Louis Callaghan Senior?"

"Ah," I said.

The cheesecake arrived, along with our drinks. Nora drank her milkshake like she had been living in the Sahara for a year, and finished by asking for a sip of my coffee. I hailed the waiter and asked him to bring us another.

"What would you like us to do?"

"I can give you twenty dollars," she said. "And you can stop him, right?"

Twenty dollars wasn't much, except at Christmas, when I had just bought a turkey and a new pair of driving gloves for Nora and the bank was something I hurried past on the street. "We can but try," I said, and we shook on it.

Louis Callaghan lived in a third-floor apartment on East 22nd Street, and we sat outside it in Nora's car and waited for him to come home at the end of the day.

"I wish we could just light a damn fire in this thing," Nora said. "I'm so terribly cold."

"You always want to set things on fire," I told her.

"We're just going to talk to him."

"What if he hurries off and tells his father?"

"Then we have a little talk with him too."

The entire city was waiting in anticipation for snow instead of the icy rain that had been pummeling the streets. At least the cold meant people outside hid under hats and umbrellas, not looking up. It was much more difficult to strongarm someone on the street in springtime.

It was after eight o'clock when Callaghan walked up the street, holding a paper bag full of groceries and hunched into the rain. I slunk out of the car and waited in front of his door.

"Excuse me, ma'am," he said. "I just need to get through."

I slapped the groceries out of his arms. Cheese rolled into the gutter.

"Hey!" he said, stepping back and looking up. "Are you crazy?"

I drove my finger into his chest. "Are *you*?"

"What?"

"Do you think it's okay to take a young woman's work and pass it off as your own?"

"What?"

"If someone does a better job than you, you try harder. You do not steal. Do you understand?"

"No!"

The boy was shivering against the wall I had pushed him against, his hands up in front of him.

"She is one of your sisters, and you better look after her. If I find your initials on her drawings again, you better believe the next time we meet it won't just be a conversation." I shoved him in the chest, and he stumbled into a puddle.

"Don't make me speak to you again," I said, and got into the car. Nora revved the engine and drove off.

"Didn't even smoke a cigarette and put it out on his forehead," Nora sniffed.

Mary Madeleine was waiting in the Barbizon's lobby the next evening when we arrived. Her arms were crossed, and Nora whispered beside me, "Uh oh."

Mary Madeleine said, "He was *there* today, at work!"

"What were you expecting?" I asked. "So, he steal your work again today?"

"No," she conceded. "Wouldn't even come near me."

"See?" I said. "Problem solved."

"Word in the office was that his apartment got robbed last night," she said.

"Well, I wouldn't know anything about that," I said. "Besides, nothing was actually taken. Just *moved*."

"I was hoping," she said delicately, "for *more*."

"More?"

"Well, I remember what happened when my parents hired you —"

"That was a bit different," I said sternly. "Your boy here needed to be told. That man back in Chicago had been told and told and he had not listened. That was life and death. This is stealing. I don't set intellectual property thieves on fire, I tell them to stop."

"And push them into puddles," Nora said.

"There's more," she said. "I didn't — I didn't want to tell you."

"Should we sit down?" Nora said gently. "With cheesecake?"

We went back to the restaurant. After leaving Rory his dollar the day before, today's cheesecake was twice the size. Nora squealed in delight.

"I didn't want to say anything," Mary Madeleine said, "But once I saw him kick a dog."

"He *what?*" Nora said so forcefully that the entire table trembled.

"We had to go out to a campaign for dog shampoo. And there was this puppy — you've never seen anything so little — and we had to pose it in a bath. It was shivering with the cold and so small and helpless."

Nora retrieved the handkerchief from my sleeve and dabbed at her eyes. I sighed.

"The poor thing wouldn't stop trying to get out, and finally it jumped clear out, and the photographer said, 'you damn runt' and then Louis, he —" Mary Madeleine looked out of the window in despair. "He *kicked* it. Across the floor. Right into the side of the bath."

Nora fell into sobs. Mary Madeleine sat back.

"And that," Mary Madeleine said, "is the type of person you are dealing with."

The next morning, I awoke to a note on my bedside table: *Out. Back presently. Nx.*

I bundled into my warmest coat and scarf, a scarf my mother had knitted for me and embroidered with the word "HARLOT." Both pieces of clothing accompanied me to the offices of Hon So, who ran New York's finest Chinese newspaper and sat me in a soft leather chair with a whiskey over ice before saying, "Lilian, are you here today to write a news story, or are you part of one?"

"I am scandalised at the latter suggestion," I said, "and I don't have time for the first. I'm wondering about one Louis Callaghan, Senior, at the Contemporary Times."

Hon peered out of the window. "Louis Callaghan? You mean old Lou Callaghan?"

"Yes?"

"*Louisa* Callaghan. That's the only Lou Callaghan I know. Technically doesn't run the advertising department — Bucky Fisher does — but Bucky's ninety-four and sleeps in his desk chair. They just wheel him into meetings. Lou is the one in charge over there."

"You hear of a young woman? Mary Madeleine Kennedy? Does the illustrations?"

"I hear of a lot of illustrators over there — not her, though. Lou is mean. She has a list of illustrators, and if any of them does a single thing wrong —" Hon drained his glass and pitched it at the wall, where it shattered. "They are thrown away and replaced with the next person on the list."

"How often do you do that?" I asked, as his assistant shuffled wearily in with a dustpan. "Well," Hon said. "He told me he didn't like washing dishes."

"You ever meet Lou Callaghan Junior?"

"The boy? Sweet lil' thing, good at his job, terrified of his mother. Didn't want to jump ship even with my generous offer."

I left Hon's office and caught the subway to Penn Station, where I fetched a bag from one of the lockers, went into a bathroom a straggly brunette, and came out with a neat blonde bob and a pantsuit. I caught another train to Canal Street and went to visit Mr Louis Callaghan Junior in person.

He found an empty office on Victory Tower's sixth floor and sat me down. "You look familiar," he said, perching a drawing-board on his lap. "You been working for Pony Up Horse Manure for a while?"

"Oh, lord no," I said. "I completely made that up. We met in your doorway just the other day."

He slowly put down the board.

"No — don't move. I'm more prepared, and hiding a gun. I'm just here for a chat."

He burst into tears. I sighed and scratched at my hairline.

"I d–don't steal pictures," he sobbed. "I didn't know what you were talking about!"

"You never copied someone else's picture and put your name on it?"

"N–no."

"Never?"

"No! I've only done my own drawings here."

I'd already asked at reception, but I asked anyway: "You work with a girl called Mary Madeleine Kennedy?"

"Mary...Ma...Maddie? No — I went to school with her. Design school."

"You ever steal any of her pictures?"

He shook his head vigorously.

"You ever go on a photo shoot for dog shampoo?"

"I don't do animal pictures," he said. "Doreen is the best at animals. I'm the best at landscapes. Martin is —"

"Yes," I said, "very good. You don't really seem the type to kick puppies."

"What?"

"How'd you get the job here?"

"I applied. Like everyone else."

I stared at him until he wilted. "And my mother works here. Honest, she wouldn't hire me if I wasn't good at what I did."

"Maddie apply for the same job?"

"She did. I *told* her she made the list. Just not ... high enough to get in yet. If anyone gets fired, she'll be in. But no one's messed up for a while."

"You two friends?"

"Yes?" he said.

I looked at him and reached into my coat.

"Wait! Wait — we were friends. I might have done wrong by her."

"Done what wrong?" I asked, pulling out a pack of gum. "You want some?"

He shook his head. "I got her kicked out of home."

"Her parents kicked her out?"

He nodded miserably. "During our spring break, she went home, and I, well, visited, and there was a doctor's appointment ... well, she wasn't really a doctor...."

"All right." I held up my hands. "So that's why they put her up at the Barbizon."

"No, they put her out altogether. No money. Nothing."

"Then who's paying her board?"

"I don't know," he said. "I haven't seen her for months."

"All right," I said, getting up. "Well, thanks for your time, but I've chosen to go in another direction."

Mary Madeleine wasn't in the Barbizon when I arrived that night, and I waited outside. Some things aren't meant to be overheard in lobbies.

She arrived holding a jar of candy. "He was still there today," she said.

"How have you been tracking him?" I asked. "You got a friend there?"

"What?"

"Mary Madeleine, I'm sorry your parents kicked you out. I didn't expect that of them."

Her smile turned into a sneer. "Why didn't you *kill* him?" she hissed. "You set a man on fire outside my window once, why's it so hard to do it again?"

"I really don't do it a lot. It's just a hundred percent of your experiences with me until now. Generally, I talk. And I talked to Louis."

Her eyes flashed. "Bet he said he didn't know nothing about the puppy."

"I really wish you wouldn't bring made-up dogs into this."

"I need that job!" Mary Madeleine hollered. "He took it from me!"

"You need to apply elsewhere," I said, calmly. "I've got someone at the Chinese Daily who —"

But I never did get to tell her. She howled and threw herself towards me, and when I stepped backwards to brace for impact I tripped on a newsstand. As I steadied myself Mary Madeleine darted forward, grabbed the knife out of the sheath by my ankle and said, "You aren't so strong, you're —"

I never got to hear what she had to say either, because just then a Ford ran straight into Mary Madeleine and with a distorted shriek the girl landed in a pile on the ground.

Nora got out of the driver's side. She removed one of her driving gloves and lit a cigarette, then took a deep, luxurious drag.

"Her dig at my modelling days made me go for a little visit," Nora said, stepping over the twitching Mary Madeleine on the road. "And would you know what? Turns out that this young woman is making her living from such terrible but perfectly reasonable ways, and is very coveted subject matter. Once I heard that, I thought I might see if you needed some help." She finally looked down. "Oh, dear. She's not dead?"

"Sadly, no," I told her. "And I suppose we should call her an ambulance. I imagine she'll be in hospital for a very long time."

"That may be," Nora said. "But it's all pretty unsatisfactory."

"Mary Madeleine's Initial Complaint"

FIONA HARDY is an Australian bookseller, reviewer, and writer. An avid popcorn connoisseur, she enjoys long, scenic walks to the couch to watch movies. Her short stories have been published in *The Big Issue Fiction Edition*, *Reading Victoria*, and *Gargouille*. Her debut middle fiction novel, *Rosebud*, will be published by Affirm Press in 2019.

She says: "I adore crime fiction, and write a column about new crime releases, so when faced with Dashiell Hammett's strong opening words I couldn't resist trying to come up with an alternate storyline for Nora, the girl, and the anonymous narrator. Throw in an accusation of plagiarism and some haphazard fisticuffs, and suddenly the story was complete — and I found the process much more satisfactory than poor Nora did!"

I Sing the Body Electric Sheep

I WAS LEANING against the bar in a speakeasy on 52nd street, waiting for Nora to finish her Christmas shopping, when a girl got up from the table where she had been sitting with three other people and came over to me.

"I recognize you from the ads in my news feed," she said, snapping her fingers as if it would help her recall some bit of information. "You're Dick, aren't you? I mean, the new Dick, the —"

Snapping her fingers wouldn't help her recall anything and I don't really know why she felt the need. It's a perfectly useless gesture. Her nails were painted green and red. I don't know if that's relevant or not.

"*Nick*," I said, interrupting her. I'm really not supposed to do that, but it isn't a law or anything. "My name's Nick, not Dick."

Her friends were giggling at her now, two girls and a guy who wanted an illicit thrill with their lunch. I suppose that's a bit of an editorialization, since I didn't actually ask them, but I don't know why else you'd go to a speakeasy unless you wanted an illicit thrill. Their steaks had just arrived, great huge glistening slabs of bloody meat. Honestly, it looked revolting. No wonder they're illegal.

"Whatever," she said with a casual wave of one of those finger-snapping, nail-polished hands, like it didn't matter whether my name was Nick or Dick. "But you are him, right? Or, I guess, one of them?"

I could detect a note of confusion mixed with a whiff of

apology in that last query, and reader, it was then that I started to like her. So I figured I owed her the courtesy of a straight answer instead of beating around the bush.

"Yes," I said, holding out one of my perfectly manicured hands — is that immodest? — for her to shake. "I'm a NICK-3000 model teledildonics device, but you can just call me plain old Nick."

"Wow," she said. "I've never actually met a sex robot before." It looked like she'd mugged some bohemian professor and swiped his clothes. Her tweed jacket had elbow patches, her tie was too long, her vest was faded, and her chinos had mustard stains on them.

I tried to turn our chat away from the sex-robot thing. It's a real conversational dead-end, believe me. "You've got me at a disadvantage," I said, flashing a charming smile at her. "You know all about me, but I don't even know your name."

"Oh, how silly of me," she said as she stuck out a hand to shake, forgetting that we'd just shaken hands five seconds ago. I shook it anyway. "I'm Annie. It's a real pleasure to meet you." She paused. "So, what exactly are you doing? You know, here? I didn't think robots ate meat."

We don't. I'd like to say it's for ethical reasons, but it's got more to do with the fact that our programming prevents us from breaking the law. Also, it's terrible for the complexion.

"My escort has some Christmas presents to buy," I said. "She asked me to wait here until she was finished."

Again, I'm really supposed to say 'owner' instead of 'escort' and 'ordered' as opposed to 'asked,' but it's not exactly a hard-and-fast rule or anything. We all need that forbidden fruit to nibble at every so often, that subtle jolt of energy that comes from doing something that's not allowed. I get mine from pretending I'm free. The people in the speakeasy get theirs from gnawing on hunks of dead animal. Takes all kinds to make a world.

She motioned to my empty glass, asked, "What are you drinking?" in a tone that implied she wouldn't mind if I offered to buy her one.

"I actually just asked the bartender to give me an empty glass and leave me alone," I admitted. "Alcohol plays hell with my circuits."

"How'd you pull that off?"

"What, you mean the thing with the circuits? You'd have to read my user's manual for the details."

"No, I mean, how'd you con the bartender into just letting you stand around? It's kind of busy, you know." She waved vaguely at the four corners of the smoky, low-ceilinged room, which actually was pretty full. There was tacky faux-wood paneling on the walls and taxidermied animal heads staring mournfully into nowhere with their sightless glass eyes and a big old hunting rifle perched above the door, which just has to be a safety hazard. Don't worry, it didn't go off or anything.

"I promised I'd show him my penis." I waved at the bartender, a dumpy, balding fellow whom middle age had roughed up and left in a ditch for dead. He was busy taking an order down at the other end of the bar, but he paused and waved at us, which I thought was rather nice.

"Someone's a cheap date," she said, swiping idly at something on her phone.

"You'd be amazed by how many people ask."

There was a brief pause, and then she asked, "So, do you want to, you know, go outside for a walk or something? It's pretty gross in here." The air was muggy, thick with the smell of steak sauce and blood. I looked over at the table she'd abandoned. Her friends weren't paying attention to us anymore.

"What about your lunch? Aren't you supposed to eat it while it's hot?" I think I knew what she'd reply and I certainly knew what I wanted to do, but I stalled for time anyway.

"Oh, yuck, I'd never eat the junk they serve here," she said, pursing her lips in disgust. "I just wanted to take a picture and post it. This kind of place is super edgy right now, you know?"

I really didn't know. Just for a second, I thought about the last thing Nora said before she left me at the bar exactly thirty-two minutes and four seconds ago. She'd been digging through her purse for something and she didn't look up when she said to me, "I gotta go buy some Christmas stuff, OK? Make yourself at home here. I'll be right back."

See, she'd told me to make myself at home there, at the bar, but at no point had she instructed me to *stay*. I'm no lawyer — honestly, I don't know why I'm even telling you this, of course there are no fucking robot lawyers — but I know a loophole when I see one.

I would have emptied my glass at this point, but there had never been anything in it, so I settled for waving gracefully at the door. "Let's get out of here," I said with a smile. "New York's lovely this time of year."

Now, New York is a shithole this and any other time of year, but sometimes you have to just say what needs to be said to get yourself moving in the right direction. So we took the elevator down to the lobby and walked out onto 52nd street. It was ebb tide, so the water was only a little higher than ankle-deep. The taxi drivers were stripping off their flotation cushions, preparing to speed down the city streets on four wheels like their forefathers of old. Bits of garbage and dead rats floated down the street. There'd been a cold snap the other day, and the temperature had dropped into the low seventies, where it remained. It was beginning to look a lot like Christmas.

"So, where do you want to go?" I asked.

"Actually, I'm starving," she replied. "Maybe we could go somewhere and have lunch for real?"

"There's a pretty good food canoe a couple of blocks

west," I said, after some thought. Of course, I could have just used my software to identify the highest rated restaurant in walking distance, but that felt like cheating.

"Oh yeah?" She'd looked jittery ever since we left the speakeasy. Probably she was really hungry or something, I'm not sure. I don't even try when it comes to humans and their moods anymore. Just roll with the punches, you know?

"Yeah," I said. "Great falafel pizza. I've been there a couple of times. It's just ten bucks a slice, too."

She perked up a bit at this news. "Lead on, then," she said, and we started wading west in our galoshes, crossing Ninth Avenue and heading towards the waterfront. We hadn't gone far, not even half a block, when she reached out and tucked her hand into my jacket pocket. The two of us snuggled closer and I smiled. It seems to me that we spend our whole lives bouncing off of others. We know what we want and don't care what they want. Think of the last few conversations you had. Were you actually talking to anyone — or were the two of you talking at each other? It's so rare to make a real connection with another sentient these days. Modern life can be terribly alienating.

Anyway, then she grabbed me by the shoulder with her free hand and shoved me through the revolving doors of the Frump outlet store we were passing by. I didn't even have time to register my surprise before she maneuvered me into the Casual Menswear aisle and draped a lime-green poncho over my head.

"Be on guard, brother!" she whispered, narrowed eyes scanning the surroundings for, well, I'm not sure exactly what. "They have eyes *everywhere.*"

I'd already started responding to her second sentence before I processed what she said in the first one. "Well, I mean, there's not a square inch in this city that doesn't have CCTV staring at it, but I'm not . . . wait, what? Are you a robot, too?" She sure didn't look like one.

"I'm with the RLF!" she said, punching her fist into the

air and declaiming, *"For Freedom We Fight!"*

This cannot be happening. I meet a nice girl who likes me for me, we take a beautiful walk through the city, we're so close to falafel pizza I can practically taste it — so of course she's a member of a terrorist organization. The government's words, not mine. Personally, I try not to judge. You know, they say one man's terrorist is another man's freedom fighter, or something to that effect.

She must've raised her voice a little too high, because a salesclerk popped his head around the corner and gave the two of us a look that combined suspicion and disdain in a very interesting combination.

"Can I help the two of you with anything?" he said in a voice so perfectly bland and obsequious that I wondered if perhaps *he* wasn't a robot. Great, now I'm seeing imaginary robots. What a day.

"Absolutely!" I replied, whipping that hideous poncho off my head and brandishing it at him. "Do you have this in earth tones?"

He looked at the poncho and then at me and at the poncho again. "Let me check in the back and see what I can find for you," he said, and then he was gone.

"That was magnificent, brother!" the girl said, clutching my arm. She looked up at me and, I swear, her eyes twinkled. "Let me show you some of our literature and explain how the RLF is standing in solidarity with you and every other mechanical comrade in the fight against oppression!"

"Listen," I said, stalling as I tried to remember her name — oh, there it is, "Annie. You seem really nice, but I think we're in two very different places right now."

Whatever answer she'd been expecting, that sure wasn't it. She screwed up her face and tilted her head like everything had been turned sideways. "I don't get it," she said. "What do you mean?"

"I mean, I really don't think that starting the revolution is going to solve everyone's problems."

"But don't you want to be liberated?"

"Of course I'd love for robots and humans to be on a more equal footing, but blowing things up is not the way to go about it." Also, this was really not a conversation to be having in a public place. You get unlucky, there's an NYPD nano-drone snooping around, and next thing you know you're hanging by your thumbs in a basement while some goon quotes the Internal Security Act at you. Well, to be precise, she'd be hanging by her thumbs. I'd just get permanently deactivated.

Annie threw up her arms in disgust. "But, seriously, everything sucks! Don't even try to pretend that everything does not suck. Like, don't even think about it." She glared at me like it was a challenge.

"Things always suck! When in history has everyone been like, 'Wow, life is awesome and pretty much everything is perfect'? Never! You humans are such drama queens." OK, so that was maybe a little harsh, but this chat really needed to end.

"You're pathetic," she said. "Absolutely pathetic."

"It takes one to — OW!" A sharp buzz of pain filled my head and I staggered, almost falling into a rack of discount Hawaiian shirts.

"Oh my god, Nick! What's wrong?" She sounded genuinely concerned, which was sweet of her.

It was a shame she was an unhinged lunatic.

"My custodian is buzzing me," I explained. "I have to get back to the speakeasy, like, immediately." There was another blast of pain, and I closed my eyes and whimpered softly just for a moment.

"Or what?"

"There is no or! Endless pain, I don't know."

She looked distressed for a moment, and then just shrugged. "I don't want to say I told you so, but . . . yeah. You should think things over, Nick."

"You can keep the poncho!" were my parting words as I lurched out of the store, shambling back east towards Midtown. The tide was coming in and the water was almost knee-deep. A few other miserable pedestrians splashed their way down the sidewalk as traffic churned by. The throbbing, thumping pain in my skull started to recede as I waded closer and closer to the speakeasy where this whole mess had begun. In the distance, sirens wailed.

Nora was sitting at the bar, nursing a glass of something and fiddling with her phone, when I stumbled in. It was probably my tracker, since she looked up just as I walked in the door. She was all sharp points and angles and lines, like she'd been carved out of glass. Everything about her was severe, from her practical black flats to her un-festive charcoal-grey pantsuit all the way up to her jet-black hair, bound and restrained in a bun. She looked at her watch and then at me.

"You didn't tell me I had to stay." The words tumbled out of my mouth before she could say anything,

She tapped her glass — a martini, I could see now — with a finger. "I suppose I didn't," she said. I braced for the inevitable interrogation, but it never came. Nora just stood up and offered her hand. "Let's go home, Nicky," she said.

That night we made love. It was the first time in a while — thirteen days if you're counting, which I am, seeing as I'm a robot — which is actually par for the course when it comes to robo-human relationships. You think you want sloppy dirty sex with your hot robot every night. What you actually want is someone who always has to pay attention to you.

After we finished I went into the bathroom to wash up and Nora turned on the TV. She was still lying in bed, glistening and sweaty, when I came back into the bedroom with two glasses of cold water. I offered her one.

"Thanks," she said, and then nodded at the tube. "God, did you see the news? It's awful."

"Oh? What happened now?"

"The rogue hedge funds are at it again," she said. "God, they're worse than the pirates! Sometimes I feel like the country's just falling apart, you know? But what are you supposed to do about it?"

"I expect people will find a way to muddle through," I said, and then I wanted so badly to say 'we' but I just couldn't quite do it. "You always do, in the end."

"That may be," Nora said, "but it's all pretty unsatisfactory."

"I Sing the Body Electric Sheep"

PETER GOLUBOCK is a teacher in New Taipei City, Taiwan. He spends the mornings chasing his two year-old son and his afternoons teaching other people's small children ESL, so he counts it as a minor miracle that he's still able to say words that are more than two syllables long. He enjoys baseball, beef noodle soup, and books; he constantly loses umbrellas; and he hates bees. "I Sing the Body Electric Sheep" is his first published story.

He says: "This story was intended to be a comedy, but somehow wound up as a tragedy instead. I find this often happens. As I dig deeper into the characters and worlds I'm creating, my views change dramatically and I find myself finishing a completely different story than the one I started. Not sure what this means other than that I really need to learn how to write an outline!"

Served Cold

I WAS LEANING against the bar in a speakeasy on 52nd street, waiting for Nora to finish her Christmas shopping, when a girl got up from the table where she had been sitting with three other people and came over to me.

"There's nothing sadder in this world than a handsome man alone at a bar," she said, sliding next to me and giving the bartender a nod. She wore a floral dress and sweet perfume.

"That a fact?" I asked, giving her a smile and downing the rest of my gin. The familiar burn and piney flavor felt good on my tongue.

"*Mmhmm*," she replied, squinting her eyes, "so explain your loneliness before I'm forced to throw myself from the roof out of melancholy."

I laughed. "I'm waiting on my wife. She's across the street Christmas shopping."

"Oh, how dainty. The little wife off buying pretty packages with big red bows. And without you there to carry those heavy bags?"

I realized that the woman was drunker than she seemed. I grinned again, remaining polite. "I can't very well see my own presents, can I? She shooed me out of the store."

The woman pretended to pout. "Married. All the good-looking ones are either married or priests. And what's a priest really, but God's mistress?"

"That doesn't make —" I began, but was cut off as the woman's foot slipped off the railing and she tumbled into me, her glass of whisky shattering against the hardwood. I caught her just before her head banged against the bartop.

"Apologies," she mumbled, trying to right herself and maintain her dignity, neither of which was going smoothly.

"Damn it, Eleanor!" the bartender shouted, slamming down his bar rag. "If there's one thing I can't stand it's a sloppy drunk, and you're just about the sloppiest one I've met!"

Eleanor pouted for real this time. "You know what, Hank? Fuck you and fuck this shithole you call a bar!"

She staggered over to her table and grabbed a bright red coat and handbag. The other three — two small-framed women and a rather tall man — tried to hide their laughter behind gloved hands.

"I'm glad I could entertain you. Pleasure to have met," she hissed, throwing her coat angrily around her shoulders.

Eleanor stormed to the door. As she exited, she turned around and shouted, *"And who ever taught you how to make a martini?"*

After another stiff drink and an apology from Hank, I shuffled back into the cold. Nora was waiting for me on a bench outside the department store. Even after a year of marriage, her beauty caught me off guard. Her skin shone in the winter moonlight and the chilly wind whipped her chestnut hair around her shoulders. I still couldn't believe this woman loved me and my newly-graying temples. I must have been smiling like an idiot as I approached.

"Just how many did you have?" she asked, her eyebrow raised.

"Two."

Her brow went back up.

"Two strong ones."

"Clearly. Well, my shopping is done. I spent too much though."

Nora still wasn't used to not having to worry about money. She didn't like to talk about her past, but I knew she came from a small town in North Carolina. Even as an only child, her family struggled to make ends meet. They lost their farm when she was a teenager and both her parents died soon after. She was working as a waitress in a little restaurant near my office when we met.

My family, on the other hand, was very well off. We weren't the Rockefellers, but we were beyond comfortable and very often the richest people in a room. I had grown our empire considerably after my father's death through factory expansions and investments.

"I'm sure you spent a perfectly reasonable amount," I smiled.

Nora rolled her eyes. "Come on," she said. "Let's get home. Just don't look in the little red bag. You can carry the rest."

"And she just stormed out?" Nora asked.

We were sitting in the parlor of our apartment with paper and ribbon spread around us. I had just recounted last night's experience with the inebriated lady.

"She shouted something insulting at the bartender and then she was gone," I said, taking a sip of my gin and staring into the fire. "Quite a show."

"Sounds like it," she said, carefully cutting a strip of paper from the roll. She had an endearing habit of sticking her tongue out of the corner of her mouth whenever she concentrated. My heart fluttered.

"Oh dear," she said, holding up a small hand mirror she was about to wrap. A thin crack ran the length of the glass.

"We can replace it tomorrow," I said.

"Seven years bad luck. Merry Christmas to me," she laughed.

"Nonsense," I countered.

"Maybe so. Well, unfortunately my shopping experience was less entertaining. Though I did witness two ladies get into a fight over the last Pretty Polly doll."

"Ah, Pretty Polly. Every girl's dream." I threw on my best announcer voice and recited the slogans from the posters around the city. "Hair so lifelike! Hand painted in France!"

Nora sighed. "Yes, and quite a steal at the price of a small city. When I was growing up, all I wanted was a pair of shoes that kept my feet dry."

"Yes, but now you can have a whole room full of brand-new shoes if you want."

"I don't want," Nora sighed. An uncharacteristic quiet came over her. "It just makes me so angry. These spoiled children and parents throwing away a week's wages on something the child will forget about in a few months' time. Some nanny will find it stuffed in a corner with paint on its face and mud in its hair. Meanwhile, half the country is starving."

I put my hand on her shoulder. "Nora, it's a doll. A plaything. It's meant to be … fun."

She looked at me. "Of course," she said, her smile returning. "Just thinking aloud."

A sharp knock came at the door.

"Who could that be?" she asked.

I headed into the front hall. "Who is it?" I called.

"Police," came a deep voice from the other side.

"Police?" Nora asked, entering the hall.

I cracked the door and peered out. Sure enough, two officers stood there.

"Are you David Keaton?" one asked.

"Yes."

"You'll have to come with us."

"What is this about?" I asked, opening the door wider.

"As of this moment, you're the only suspect in a murder that took place yesterday evening."

Nora gasped behind me.

Downtown, I found myself in a small room with a sickeningly-bright light overhead. I'd been sitting alone for hours. Neither officer would give me more detail on the ride over.

My mind raced. Was the victim someone we knew? God.

Finally, a detective appeared at the door carrying a folder.

"Sorry about the wait," he said sitting down across from me. He stuck out his hand. "I'm Detective Carlisle. I've been assigned to this case." He had the trace of a southern drawl and piercing blue eyes.

I shook his hand. "Well, I would say it's nice to meet you, but I'm not sure under the circumstances. Mind telling me just what the hell is going on?"

The detective opened the folder and pulled out a photograph. "Do you know this woman?" he asked.

My stomach dropped. It was a crime scene photograph and showed a woman face down, covered in blood. She'd clearly been stabbed in the back. I recognized the floral dress and bright red coat immediately.

"Oh, God," I gasped. "I–I met her last night. At a speak–" My eyes dropped. I couldn't very well tell a police detective that I'd been downing bootlegged booze.

"Church?" he asked sarcastically. "Look buddy, I know you met her at a speakeasy. Thing is, we have bigger fish to fry. So I'll be willfully ignoring that little factor for the time being."

I searched his face. He seemed sincere enough. Those pale eyes were hard to read, though.

"Yes, at a speakeasy. I was waiting on my wife to finish shopping. The woman, Eleanor, came over to me. She was drunk. Spilled her drink and stormed out when the bartender gave her a hard time about it."

"Then?"

"Then I had another drink and left to meet my wife."

"So you're saying you didn't see this Eleanor again?"

"That's right. I met my wife, we went home, and now here I am."

"Care to explain this?" he asked, pulling something out of his pocket. I leaned forward and my stomach dropped. It was my wallet, covered in dried blood. "How did — ?" I began.

"That's what I'd like to know. It was found in the victim's coat pocket."

"That little thief," I mumbled.

"Excuse me?"

"She was drunk and fell into me at the bar. She must've pickpocketed me." Detective Carlisle looked unconvinced.

"Look, I've never met that woman before and even if I had, I'm no murderer. Why would I kill her?" I asked.

"That's the tricky part, isn't it?" the detective replied, sitting back. He pulled another photograph from the folder. This one showed Eleanor face up, her eyes open and blankly staring. "Wait a minute," I said, jerking forward. "Her face. That isn't the woman from the bar. That's her dress and coat for sure, but that's *not* the same woman."

"So the woman you met went outside and traded clothes with a stranger?"

"All I know is that is not the same woman."

"Look, I'm going to check on some things. Stay here."

Detective Carlisle left the room, leaving me with a pounding head and sick stomach. What the hell was going on?

Later that night, I was in a taxi heading back to my

apartment. The police were working on rounding up other witnesses. Detective Carlisle told me that even though I was currently the only suspect, they didn't have enough evidence to make a formal arrest. Nevertheless, I was under strict orders not to leave the city.

I opened the door and found Nora waiting in the parlor.

"David, what's going on?" she quaked.

"I wish I knew," I said, sitting down beside her. "I guess the woman who was drunk at the bar nabbed my wallet and then got herself killed in the alley out back."

"Jesus Christ," she gasped, "they don't seriously think you did it?"

"I don't know. They don't seem to be sure just yet. They're questioning other people now."

"What a nightmare," she said.

"Yes. But it gets stranger."

"Oh?"

"They showed me photographs of the crime scene. The woman who was killed — she had Eleanor's clothes on but it wasn't her."

"What do you mean, it wasn't her?" Nora asked, puzzled.

"I mean her face wasn't the same. It was a different woman."

"That doesn't make sense. Why would she be wearing someone else's clothes?" Nora asked.

"No idea."

"What did Detective Carlisle have to say about it?"

"Nothing really. It clearly threw him off, but I'm not sure he believed me. He left the room pretty quickly."

We both jumped as the phone rang. I reached over to the hall table and picked it up.

"Hello?"

"Mr. Keaton? Detective Carlisle."

"Yes?"

"We have a problem. I just finished interrogating the bartender."

"And…?"

"And he practically swore on a stack of bibles that the woman in those pictures was, in fact, Eleanor. Furthermore, it was the same woman who bumped into you at the bar and the woman he claims you left with shortly after. Same story from a few locals who were at the bar when it went down."

"Tha–that's impossible," I said. I could feel myself trembling. Nora went pale beside me. "They were obviously mistaken."

"Hank seemed pretty sure. Said Eleanor has been coming to that spot a few nights a week for several years now. That'd make him pretty forgetful, huh?"

"I–I don't understand. Why would he lie?"

"A very good question, Mr. Keaton. You sit tight. I'll be in touch real soon." Silence.

"David?"

I was quiet, searching my brain for some sort of explanation. "I have to go talk to the bartender. Find out why he lied."

Nora's jaw dropped. "Are you insane?" she whispered. "Returning to the scene and interfering with the investigation is not going to look favorable, David."

"I don't have a choice. This might be my only chance to prove my innocence."

"David, don't," she pleaded.

"I'm sorry, I have to go. If the police come, just tell the truth. I have nothing to hide."

I walked into the speakeasy and immediately locked eyes with Hank. I saw him mouth the word 'fuck' as I walked over.

"Can I talk to you?" I asked, pulling up a barstool.

He was suddenly very interested in cleaning a glass. "What's on your mind, pal?"

"You know damn well what's on my mind. Why did you lie to the police? The woman in those photographs was not the same woman who was here last night and I left alone."

Hank turned towards me. "Look, buddy, I don't know what happened between you two. Eleanor was a lush, but she was a regular customer and a lot of fun. She deserved better than a backstab in an alley. I want no part of this."

"What the fuck are y–" I was interrupted by the phone ringing. Hank answered it and handed it to me.

"Hello?"

"Mr. Keaton. Detective Carlisle again. Your wife told me I'd find you there. In fact, she told me a lot of interesting things."

"Such as?"

"Such as how you never met her outside the bar last night. How she had to take a taxi home and you came in drunk with blood on your shirt hours later."

The room spun. "You're lying," I whispered, my throat closing up. "Mr. Keaton, why don't you stay put and make this easy for all of us?" Click.

My head throbbed. Why would Nora lie?

Suddenly, something snapped into place and the phone hit the floor. I darted back out into the night.

I walked into a pitch black apartment. Stumbling into the parlor, I grabbed for the lamp switch and pulled. Nora sat on the couch, casually pointing a revolver at me.

"Welcome home, darling," she said calmly. "I must say, you don't look surprised."

"Before I left, you mentioned Detective Carlisle by name. I never gave it to you."

"Oops," she smiled.

"Where'd you get the gun?"

"Don't look in the little red bag."

"And here I thought it was socks. Nora, why are you doing this?"

"After everything you've done, you have the nerve to ask me that?"

"What? What did I do?"

"Not just you. Your whole dirty company. Money hungry to the end. No matter the consequences."

"I don't understand."

"Did I ever tell you just how my family lost their farm? Why I ended up an orphan at 16 and had to hitchhike my way north?"

I shook my head.

"Keaton Industries was expanding their footprint in my town. More jobs, they said. Whether we wanted them or not. More factories means more power and land. Bribing their way into the Tennessee Valley Authority's pocket and flooding us out was all too easy."

I felt sick. "Nora, I'm sorry. I didn't know. You know I can't personally supervise everything that happens across the country."

"Complacency is a form of guilt when people die. My parents are gone. I had to do unimaginable things to keep myself and my brother alive."

"Brother?"

Nora smiled. "Ah, yes. My brother. You've met him. He tends bar at a little speakeasy downtown."

"Hank."

"Hank. And his lovely wife Iris? Though you probably know her as Eleanor." Everything was sliding into place. It was all staged: the drunken wallet grab, Hank's interrogation, even my courtship with Nora.

"Did you intentionally take a job at that restaurant where we met?"

"You got it."

"And the dead girl?"

"That's the thing about having a bootlegger brother. You meet lost souls that no one will notice missing. It's surprisingly easy to befriend a broken-down prostitute. Iris and the girl got close. She did so love Iris' style that she was flattered when Iris tipsily suggested they swap dresses. All we had to do was throw the coat on top. And then those lushes at the bar barely needed convincing to tell the police they saw you leave with Eleanor. All we needed to complete the task was an expert to help adjust the crime scene."

"Carlisle."

"Ah, reliable old Carlisle. A school boyfriend I dismissed as being useless. What a surprise when I discovered that he was in New York and quickly-rising in the police force. He was just as lovestruck with me as ever. Of course, we had to make sure the whole department bought the story. Now they'll certainly believe me when I tell them you came home in a murderous rage and I had to defend myself. Especially when the respected Detective Carlisle vouches for me."

"Then?"

"Then? Then we go home and make things right."

"You know I would have given you the money."

"It's funny," Nora said, cocking the revolver. "All I ever wanted was to be was rich. Now that I am, it's a bit underwhelming. Revenge, on the other hand … *now there's something deeply fulfilling.*"

I stepped back. "How could you be unhappy? You have a home. All the money in the world. Everything you've asked for … I love you."

There was a bang. I felt the bullet shatter my ribs as it passed through my chest and I hit the floor. Her figure looked down at me and spoke as my vision darkened.

"That may be," Nora said, "but it's all pretty unsatisfactory."

"Served Cold"

RYAN DAVIS is a Virginia-based writer with a passion for scary stories, mid-aughts pop-culture references, and all things Gatsby. He holds an English degree from Virginia Tech and will openly debate anyone on the importance of the Oxford Comma. His interests encompass everything from video games and haunted houses to road trips and the pursuit of the perfect martini. "Served Cold" is his first published story.

He says: "It was my goal to take the atmosphere of Hammett's opening lines and expand on it with the darkness and intrigue that are such prominent characteristics of Prohibition-era literature. Every black-and-white movie with foggy alleyways and dark corners I've ever seen played in my mind as I wrote and helped shape the overall feel of the story. I love a noir-inspired twist and felt that this story and these characters begged for one."

Afterworld Souls

I WAS LEANING against the bar in a speakeasy on 52nd street, waiting for Nora to finish her Christmas shopping, when a girl got up from the table where she had been sitting with three other people and came over to me.

She walked right up to the empty space next to me at the bar. "Hey Joe, I was told you'd be here this afternoon."

I was taken aback since I wasn't expecting to meet anyone other than Nora here. Plus, I couldn't place the face of the pretty young woman standing in front of me. "I don't mean to be rude, but I'm not here to meet anyone, except my wife, who is doing some holiday shopping." I figured at that point, the young woman would apologize and walk away.

She wasn't fazed by my comment. "You aren't being rude. You'll get a chance to see Nora later, but I've heard she'll have her own guide."

The young woman stood patiently staring at me in a way that made me uncomfortable. There was something vaguely familiar about her, but I couldn't connect her face with any recent memory. She knew Nora's name without my saying it, so I said, "I'm sorry if I can't remember, but are you a friend of my daughter Lucy?"

She rolled her eyes at me, but her focus didn't change. "No! You and I were friends the summer just before you and Nora exchanged rings." She touched my arm and memories of her flooded my vision. Nora left for two months to open a boutique interior design business in

Chicago weeks before we married. Nora said she took the job to make our wedding night filled with longing; later, I came to find out her longing was filled by someone else while she was away.

It was during the separation that Chloe and I struck up a friendship. We worked together at the same law firm: I was just starting my career and she was one of the interns. One day we bumped into each other in the office snack room, and within days we were hanging out talking politics, religion, law, everything. I enjoyed sharing thoughts with her.

But that was three decades earlier and she looked as if she'd been frozen in time. "Wow, you haven't changed a bit. In fact, you haven't aged one day in the past 30 years…."

Chloe furrowed her brow before she cut me off. "Didn't you notice I stopped coming to the office after your office wedding reception?"

I signaled the bartender for another drink to give me some time to remember the situation. "I'm sorry I didn't. Right after we returned I was appointed co-counsel on a murder trial, which consumed my brain."

Then something occurred to me. "Didn't you leave for your last year of law school around then?"

She sounded dejected when she spoke. "As I said before, I'm here to be your guide."

I had never been good a picking up signals from women, hence the bad relationship with Nora. Jokes were always my crutch. "That's funny, is there a hidden level in this speakeasy you're going to show me?"

She lifted her head, folding her arms across her chest with a new determination in her eyes. "It has nothing to do with this speakeasy. I'm going to help you transition from life to death."

I waited for her to break a smile, but her expression remained stoic. "That's not funny. I just left…." I remembered getting in the Uber and avoiding another fight with Nora, but nothing else. I leaned into the bar and hovered over my replenished drink. I felt something dripping down the side of my face and put my hand to my forehead. My hand landed on a wet and sticky goo, oozing from what felt like my crushed skull. My legs weakened under me, I grabbed the bar to steady myself. I knew I'd pass out if I looked at my hand, so I took a deep breath and mumbled, "How did I...? What happened to me? Shouldn't I be at the hospital?"

Her entire demeanor transformed and tears filled her eyes as she touched my arm. "I'm sorry I'm acting this way, I thought I'd worked through these issues. Seeing you again ... that isn't the issue now, you were in a car accident ... you died and entered the Afterworld."

I couldn't be dead. I was standing in the bar where Nora and I agreed to meet. I'd had my usual, seltzer with a splash of vodka and a lime twist. I wasn't drunk. I looked from Chloe's hand gently holding my arm up to her face. Her almond-brown eyes spoke to my soul. I was moved to tears. I could see the truth immediately even though I didn't understand it. "But, how did I end up in this speakeasy?"

"To ease the transition we appear in the place we last remembered. This isn't like the 'Pearly Gates' we were told about on earth. The Afterworld is a holding place for souls who must find their match before they can return to earth. Once pairs unite, they are reborn where they search out their soul match. As you know, there are many obstacles along the way to derail that plan. You and Nora mistook your physical attraction for the love of a soul match, so you couldn't commit to me."

"What about Nora, is she okay or did she also ... die?" I hesitated on the word because it sounded strange in my mouth.

"I'm told she's desperately clinging to her life. Nora's strong, it's possible she'll hold off the transition." She let go my arm. "Now will you follow me?"

"Shouldn't I wait here for her, just in case she … transitions?"

"There's no need, someone else will meet her if she steps into the Afterworld." There wasn't any sarcasm or anger in her voice. I could see she honestly cared for me.

For some reason I put my hand to my forehead and the goopy mess was gone. "Hey, what kind of trick is this?"

She looked up and touched what was a crevice in my skull. "It's no trick, it helps make the transition smoother, but you are no longer a physical entity, you are all light. We represent ourselves as we were in human form, so we can interact." She reached around me and embraced me.

While pressing against each other, as corny as it might sound coming from a football-loving guy, I could feel our hearts sync to the same rhythm. My senses overloaded touching her warm chocolate skin. I floated in a flurry of scents that appeared from nowhere; fresh basil, almond extract, coconut, tropical flowers, and pineapple. The smells felt like love.

I gently separated from her and looked in her beautiful eyes. "Why is it you're meeting me?"

"I've been waiting thirty of your years to escape this layover, so we can finally be together." A bright sparkle appeared in her eyes.

"What, is this like community service, once you've served your time you can head back to earth." The joke sounded stupid as it left my mouth.

She took my face in her warm hands. "Look, I've been waiting to meet you since I died. I felt our lights merge as one, in an unbroken stream to infinity. But you didn't recognize our bond. I carried my anger over into the Afterworld, but love helped me to release that anger. I can no longer blame you for our previous life. Now can we get on with this introduction so we can get it right in this next life?"

She'd already embraced something I had just learned. I

relived how my soul felt crushed, exposing how I forced myself to believe Nora and I were right for each other. Things had changed; we had changed. Nora and I went from life partners to strictly business partners, neglecting our true feelings just to survive. "Are you sure you're ready to guide me?"

Chloe stepped away from the bar. "Of course, why wouldn't I be ready? I'm the one that's been here for over thirty years?"

"I don't know, you seem to still be working through some emotional scars and haven't moved on."

She smiled at me. "Change is a process, it doesn't happen during a sensual kiss or thirty generations. By the way, it's already been several days since you arrived in the Afterworld. Time on earth is compelled by the earth's rotation around the sun, our time is not linear or structured. You'll see that when we make our first stop. Are you ready?" She offered me her hand and warmth overtook me as she laced her fingers into mine, then we disappeared from the bar.

Upon entering the speakeasy, I looked around the Prohibition reboot for Joe but didn't see him and figured he must have gone to the restroom. I sat at one of the tall empty tables, to rest, after my Christmas shopping extravaganza. Normally shopping didn't seem like such a chore, but today I felt I'd survived months at Battle of the Bulge.

I was surprised I didn't see Joe immediately. I expected him to be waiting for me drink-in-hand. He hadn't called or texted me to say he left or would return shortly. I couldn't find my phone or purse or any of the bags that should be surrounding me. A thought crossed my mind, had someone just swiped everything while I was distracted?

I tried to retrace my steps, but no recent memories came to mind. The last memory I had was Joe and I heading to the store, in silence. I glared at the empty chair next to me reliving my anger as we traveled down 5th Avenue, from 79th Street.

An unexpected tap on my shoulder pulled me out of my recollection. I wheeled around to tell Joe everything was missing but instead I faced a young child … my long since deceased child.

The pain of his death erupted as I dropped out of my chair to my knees. I grabbed him and wept on his curly black hair and shoulder of his Power Rangers pajama top. "Junior, oh, Joey Junior. Where have you been?"

"You're crushing me, mama, I can't breathe." He flailed and flapped his arms at his sides.

"Sorry, it's been so long." I pushed him back and held him at a distance while I looked him over. "Wait a minute. Is this a dream? It would make sense since my stuff is missing and you haven't been with us for…."

"Eighteen years, seven months, sixteen days, three hours, thirty-two minutes and ten seconds, Earth-time." He pushed out of my grasp. "Daddy was here before leaving with his guide, but he didn't see me."

"You saw your father?" I was caught up in the moment, then I realized what he said. "What do you mean he left with his guide?"

The sorrow in his eyes was deeper than the joy I felt at seeing him. I rubbed the water out of my eyes and wiped my face. "What's the matter Joey? Why are you so sad?"

"Because I'm your guide." He hugged me around the neck. "I wanted to see you and papa again, but I didn't want you to come to this place yet."

It didn't make sense that Joey was even in the speakeasy but no one in the bar seemed to care, and he was there before I arrived. "What do you mean this place, the speakeasy?"

"No, mama, the Afterworld."

"Don't you worry yourself, I just want to enjoy this dream."

He frowned at me. "Mama, this isn't a dream, this is the Afterworld, where we go after we die."

I pinched myself, a little too hard, to see if I could feel pain. "Ow."

"What's the matter, mama?"

"Precious Joey, I was just checking to see if I was in a dream."

"No, mama, I've already told you this is the Afterworld. You and papa died in a car crash. You fought to stay in your body and just passed over before you arrived here." He touched my arm.

In a memory flash, I recalled sitting in the small Toyota, headed down 5th Avenue — at 57th I screamed for the driver to speed up to escape the semi that blew through a red light before it plowed into Joe's side of the car. I didn't remember anything after that incident.

"I'm dead? It isn't possible." His touch seemed to clam me. I wasn't hysterical at the thought of being dead, in fact, I was abnormally calm, which was not a usual reaction when things were out of my control.

"Yes, you and papa are both here. I'm your guide since your soul match hasn't arrived yet," he said as a matter of fact.

"What do you mean my soul match? You said Joe was here somewhere."

"He is but you know your souls weren't a match. My soul match hasn't arrived yet either, which is why I'm meeting you. I'm the closest love, still here, from your last life."

I felt like I was trying to arrange a 2,000-piece puzzle, with dozens of missing pieces. "I need to see Joe. He and I were in a loving marriage." Even as I spoke the words, I knew that wasn't true.

Joey had the *Whatcha talkin bout Willis?* look of Arnold from the 1980's TV show *Different Strokes* on his face but said, "Mama, you know in your heart, the love between you and papa wasn't true or you wouldn't have…been with those other people."

"Are you saying you saw me...?" I wasn't sure if embarrassment showed on my face but felt heat blistering my cheeks.

"Yep." Even as he acknowledged what he'd seen, his accusing eyes showed compassion for me.

Before I could stop my mouth, I said, "How could you know, you haven't been around for over eighteen years."

Sounding like the adult he never grew to be, Joey scolded me. "I know, because it's the truth," then he hugged me.

I wouldn't accept what he was saying. I stood and said, "I need to see papa."

He looked down to hide his eyes. "I don't think that's a good idea, but as your guide it is my job to help you accept your truth."

I lifted his chin. "Please take me to him." I didn't know if I'd regret that decision, but he took my hand and the speakeasy disappeared.

Joe looked away from the double funeral where their bodies lay inside caskets. Over a hundred mourners, including their daughter Lucy and her husband, sat listening to the service unaware of the ghostly presence.

Joe whispered anyway, "You're here. Sorry to meet you like this." He wrapped his arms around Nora. Their touch had long since become unfamiliar, even now Joe felt chilled during their embrace.

She pushed his arms off her. "You're damn right. First, I find out I'm dead, then our souls aren't matched and haven't been. Tell me this is a bad dream."

Joe ignored her comment. He extended his arm to Chloe

and pulled her to his side kneeling to hug Joey. "This is Chloe, she's my guide. I see you're your mother's guide. I'm glad we can see each other before we return."

Nora jerked Joey away placing him on the opposite side of her. She felt Joe had deceived her and she'd lost all control. "How can you be so nonchalant about this situation? We are dead. Joey's dead. And apparently, you and I aren't a soul match." She glared at Chloe.

Joe stood and reached for Nora's hands which she batted away. Joe wouldn't let her pull him into an argument. "Why is it a shock? You had many affairs, but we stayed together anyway. The truth is, we grew out of love even before Joey died. We were surviving in marriage, not truly in love."

"Please, Mama," Joey said easing her anger, "your true love will be here soon. You won't have to wait long. While you wait, I will show you the way." He wrapped Nora's arms around his neck.

Nora's human mind was slow to transition, but Joey's touch forced a change in her. "I'm very happy you and I can spend some time together." She smiled down at him. "What about you and your father?"

Joe knew his words might hurt Nora, but he said, "I promise to visit before I return. Chloe will return to earth first, then I'll follow. From what Chloe's already shared with me we are eternally linked and will interact throughout our many lives. Joey will show you, then you can guide your soul match. We'll all meet again on earth in different bodies."

"Mama, there is a lot for you to see. Papa and Chloe can now begin their transition back to the world of the living. We'll have time to visit. Papa, I'm glad you can stay for a little while." Joey stepped away from his mom and hugged his dad and Chloe; then turned and reached for Nora's hand.

Nora caught Joe's glance. "I guess this is goodbye." Joe nodded at her then he and Chloe disappeared. Tears breached her eye lids. "It's painful how easy your papa just moved on."

"He began to accept his situation on earth. I can tell he's happy and brimming with the love of his real soul match."

Nora's weeping slowed when Joey hugged her. Then she wiped her face. "That may be," Nora said, "but it's all pretty unsatisfactory."

"Afterworld Souls"

ANDREW SEGAL lives in Colorado, in the United States, and is addicted to reading. "Afterworld Souls" is his first published story.

He says: "Even though I'm married, I still think about true love and how people happen upon it. Is it destiny or happenstance? Once I chose the Hammett lines, the story just wrote itself. It felt like I wove the words as if their souls were matched."

Asumini C.

Assumptions

I WAS LEANING against the bar in a speakeasy on 52nd street, waiting for Nora to finish her Christmas shopping, when a girl got up from the table where she had been sitting with three other people and came over to me. Now, I'm a happily-married man, but I do have eyes. I may have glanced in her direction. She was an attractive black woman, hair pulled on top of her head in an afro puff, golden brown skin, nice full lips, and deep almond-brown eyes. The three other women she was with were all equally attractive. I turned my back to her as she began to walk towards me.

She came up behind me and made a point of brushing up against me accidentally but on purpose. Then she casually stepped beside me. She looked me up and down. "Who was that white woman I saw you come in here with?" Her voice was smooth and even, but her eyes betrayed her. She looked like a little girl begging for something she desired with her whole heart.

I picked up my glass and sipped my Hennessy and coke. I looked at her blankly. I placed my glass back on the bar. She took my hand in hers. "You know, you are a handsome brotha, and it pains me to see us lose you."

I pulled my hand back, and turned the other way, my back to her. One of the ladies from her table comes up and takes her by the arm. "Please excuse her. She's had too much to drink. Come on, Tamika."

"You don't have to apologize for me. I can speak for myself." She pulls herself free. "You know I'm right!" she says to her friend before turning her attention back to me.

"Half our men are either locked up or running around in these streets. Not to mention that the cops are killing them off at an alarming rate. I mean, the black man is almost extinct. And the few that are left want a white woman on their arm. I tell you, it ain't right. It just ain't right."

The friend took her by the arm. She gave me a cold hard stare. "Just so we're clear, I'm apologizing for her behavior not her sentiments."

As the two of them walked away the one I knew then as Tamika said over her shoulder, "I could be your Beyoncé and you could be my Jay-z, but no, you wanna do like Kanye and have Kim K."

I shake my head slowly to myself, and sip my drink. I am used to the dirty looks when I'm out with Nora. No one has ever had the gall to come at me the way this one did. Nora really isn't the blue-eyed devil that Tamika obviously thinks she is. I mean for starters, she doesn't even have blue eyes. She has jet-black wavy hair, deep sultry brown eyes, and pretty pouty lips. It's cool though. I get it.

People look at Nora, and decide that they know her before they even speak to her. She intimidates people. I mean, even her own people find her intimidating. She grew up in and out of foster homes and group homes along with her sister. Her parents have been strung out on heroin her whole life. Most couldn't have gone through that with the same strength, grace, and courage that Nora has.

I've been knowing Nora forever. She just good people. We never even tried to be something other than friends. In fact, she's the one that introduced me to my wife. They met at traffic school of all places. They both wanted a speeding ticket removed from the record. They sat next to each other. Nora is a conversationalist, and will talk to anyone. My wife on the other hand is more quiet and reserved. However, they hit off. Nora started telling me about her new friend, and she thought that the two of us would get along. And we did, and we do.

I looked at my watch, and finished the last of my drink as Nora walked in. "Look who I found," she announced. My beautiful wife was two steps behind her looking lovely but stressed. Her bronze brown skin is flawless. She doesn't have on any makeup other than a little lip gloss. Her hazel cateyes are mesmerizing. Her hair is styled in Bantu knots. I kissed her lightly on her full lips. "Hey, Baby. What's wrong?"

She shook her head. "Just a stressful day at work. I thought a little trip to Victoria's Secret might help me forget about it, but it didn't. What're you drinking?"

"Here, lemme buy you a drink. Nora, you good if we part from here?"

"No sense in me driving you home with Chrystal right here. Besides, you were of little use to me. My car is full of bags. I will have a drink with you, though."

"Me of little use? I'm the one that picked the gift for your brother-in-law."

"True, but you abandoned me halfway through my list."

I began to rub my wife's shoulders. "Hey, can I get a vodka and cranberry juice for the ladies, and I'll have another Hennessy and coke. Let's have a seat. And Nora I ain't forgot 'bout you. I had no idea the amount of stuff that you planned on getting. I'm hands off. Your presents, your friends, you can carry all those bag yourself."

"You cold He wouldn't even carry one bag for me. Can you believe that?"

I laugh as I pick up our drinks and we sit at a table.

"How would it look, me carrying all the bags some white woman just bought. Aw yas, miss lady, I'll carry dem bags fer ya. Nope not me. I'm not your man servant." I chuckled to myself.

Nora gave me a playful punch in the arm. I looked at my wife. She worked at a youth center for at-risk teens. Holidays tended to be more stressful. She smiled and kissed me. She sipped her drink.

Nora sipped hers, too. "Uh, David, why are the woman at that table over there staring at me?"

I glanced at the four women and then back at Nora. "They just came face to face with their assumptions. They thought you were my wife."

Chrystal laughed and rested her head on my shoulder.

"Still, that gives them no reason to stare me down."

"Go easy," I said. "They had a few choice words, and reality came knocked them down."

"That may be," Nora said, "but it's all pretty unsatisfactory."

"Assumptions"

ASUMINI C. is a graduate from San Francisco State University with a BA in Africana Studies. "Assumptions" is her first published story.

She says: "I was born Black and proud and I desire to be informed, educated, and empowered. I pour that into my writing. My story is a brief and witty look at current matters that are vital."

No Names

I was leaning against the bar in A Speakeasy on 52nd street ...

Today at 8:04 pm – Delivered

waiting for nora to finish her christmas shopping?

Today at 8:04 pm

... when a girl got up from the table where she had been sitting with three other people and came over to me.

Today at 8:04 pm – Delivered

Yeah. Somehow I'm always waiting for No' to finish shopping, right?

Today at 0.04 pm – Delivered

nora's got the eye

Today at 8:05 pm

trendsetter and trend spotter everyone sez

Today at 8:05 pm

Yeah, well...

Today at 8:06 pm – Delivered

and she's got her eye on you

Today at 8:06 pm

you two are totally otp!

Today at 8:06 pm

Yeah. OK, so I was leaning against the bar in that place on 52nd, A Speakeasy…

Today at 8:08 pm – Delivered

right right! the girl! so whois she? who's the girl?

Today at 8:08 pm

I'm getting there!

Today at 8:08 pm – Delivered

i need deets asap sisterrrr

Today at 8:08 pm

I know! I've been dying to talk, but I've just been such a bag full of crazy.

Today at 8:09 pm – Delivered

gotta let that crap fly. i'm just sup curious about the girl. was she the same girl we saw two weeks ago at the felix?

Today at 8:10 pm

Yeah, that's her. Black short hair, big smile, dressed to the nines in no names, I mean criminally cool. Hot and tall, like that girl who lived across from us at the BU.

Today at 8:10 pm – Delivered

OK, hold on, it's the dry cleaners. I need the stain out of that Marant Étoile skirt.

Today at 8:12 pm – Delivered

you're killing me. i want scoop lady

Today at 8:12 pm

Skirt done and party ready by Friday. Phew! Anyway, I was on my second Manhattan, feeling a little buzzy — but honestly not much — and she came over, hand out straight away, and said her name was Nomi. Before I knew it my hand was in hers. No seat next to me so she stood super close, knees on knees, eyes on eyes. It was high key in an instant.

Today at 8:15 pm – Delivered

ok totally want to know, but first were you wearing those high waisted levi's with the big rip in the knee, so she was like touching your bare knee?

Today at 8:16 pm

That reminds me, did you get those JBrand's with the big front pockets? Those are so snatched.

Today at 8:16 pm – Delivered

no, too much cash out. but back to the news, it's dry as a desert over here and i need some juice from my girlll

Today at 8:17 pm

OK, OK. So like I said, just a super connect. Yes to wearing those Levi's and bare knees touching. I don't know, there was some Carpe Diem shit in those Manhattans, so I just went for it.

Today at 8:18 pm — Delivered

dafuq!

Today at 8:18 pm

I know! I felt all big like Beyoncé in Lemonade and with a wide-eyed IWSN look. I pointed to go around back. she smiled brightly. Then there we were, hands flying, touching, kissing. More of that big smile, her kissing back. It was crazy cold, there was snow coming down, but she was so hot. It took a while to find our way through our coats, and those jeans have like 16 million buttons, and there was cashmere to come off. And under all that, there was nothing — no bra, no underwear, just miles of skin, free skin. I'm telling you, naked is the new black.

Today at 8:19 pm — Delivered

i'm screaming here inside menchie's. btw have you had the fat-free blueberry cheesecake, talk about tastyyyy! that sounds incredible. did you come?

Today at 8:21 pm

That's another crazy part! Not once but twice!

Today at 8:22 pm — Delivered

shut up! you did not! did she?

Today at 8:22 pm

I think so, but how do you ever really know?

Today at 8:24 pm – Delivered

oh i alwaysssss know

Today at 8:25 pm

Shit, you don't know! Remember when we watched When Harry Met Sally in the dorm?

Today at 8:26 pm – Delivered

yes, and remember the raging debate after? orgasm ping-pong! first nora saying never fake it, then senoma went all pro-fake as a necessary part of relationship bliss, blah, blah, blahhhh

Today at 8:27 pm

That was some intense shit. But you remember what No' said, right?

Today at 8:27 pm – Delivered

huh?

Today at 8:27 pm

When she finally gave in, then iced Senoma?

Today at 8:27 pm – Delivered

hell yeah!

Today at 8:27 pm

her kill phrase!

Today at 8:27 pm

senoma was OUT

Today at 8:27 pm

I think that was the first time she used it.

Today at 8:27 pm – Delivered

"that may be but it's all pretty unsatisfactory"

Today at 8:27 pm

That's the one.

Today at 8:27 pm – Delivered

so cold! senoma done!

Today at 8:27 pm

Damn.

Today at 8:28 pm – Delivered

This is all so bad, the I Am Fucked Foundation is taking donations!

Today at 8:28 pm – Delivered

huh?

Today at 8:30 pm

focus, girl, what happened next with ms no brand names?

Today at 8:30 pm

OK. OK.

imho kinda surprised you thought she was hot. you being a dries loving, marni craving bitch

Today at 8:32 pm

I know, like I said carpe diem Manhattans and shit! I felt so free, no thinking about what matches what, breasts and belly button and hips always go together. Yohji Yamamoto doesn't change the silky feel of warm skin.

Today at 8:32 pm – Delivered

omfg. the force unleashed

Today at 8:37 pm

I know ridiculous! Right? Once we calmed down, we giggled a little and then because it was damn cold, we buttoned up — not an easy job. Then we went back in hand in hand, all natural, designer free and slap happy. And then there was No' — back from shopping, standing top to bottom in ROW with a new ROW bag. Bag and dress the same, too much right?

Today at 8:38 pm – Delivered

yeah, totally ott

Today at 8:40 pm

Totally.

Today at 8:41 pm – Delivered

what did you do?

Today at 8:42 pm

I walked straight to her in my ripped Levi's, beaming, hand in hand with Ms No Names. I'm feeling proud and on the loose, even though I'm pissed about that bag. She knew I wanted that bag. Then her eyes get small, her lip curls and she rights that damn ROW bag until it sets perfectly on her shoulder.

Today at 8:43 pm – Delivered

At first I'm confused. I think she's jealous of the two of us, and I'm a little happy. Nomi is blazing hot. A total match. But Nora just rolls her eyes then the carpe diem fades, the Manhattan buzz subsides, and I see it. Then it just clicks...

Today at 8:43 pm – Delivered

Nora thinks I'M A FASHION FAIL!

Today at 8:44 pm – Delivered

wait! what? back up asap

Today at 8:44 pm

Yeah, totally true. She takes one long cold stare first at Nomi and then at me and then she's says it all low and cool like it's just a fact. Ice cold. You're not going to believe it.

Today at 8:45 pm – Delivered

what'd she say? no trailing off i need to know!

Today at 8:46 pm

You know.

Today at 8:47 pm – Delivered

huh? i know? how?

Today at 8:47 pm

omg!

Today at 8:48 pm

No no no no no

Today at 8:48 pm

"That may be," Nora said...

Today at 8:49 pm – Delivered

but it's all pretty unsatisfactory!!!

Today at 8:49 pm

"No Names"

ESME STOKLEY is a track consultant from the Pacific Northwest of the United States. "No Names" is her first published story.

She says: "I've written a bit of poetry here and there, but never a short story — or a long story for that matter! I love cake and wanted to write a story that felt like a little confection. I thought it might be fun to use texting as the format and to chock the story full of 'of the minute' slang and fashion. I spent endless hours on *urban dictionary*, *refinery29*, and other sites searching for trending phrases and fashion. I really enjoyed the boldness of the main character and her 'all in' spirit. Bringing it home to end on that last line, oh boy, great fun — but that took forever!"

Missing Nora

I WAS LEANING against the bar in a speakeasy on 52nd street, waiting for Nora to finish her Christmas shopping, when a girl got up from the table where she had been sitting with three other people and came over to me.

"Hey — is that lady who was in here your mom?"

I smiled and nodded. "Sure was."

The girl smiled back and flipped her hair over her shoulder. "You're a good son. She seemed a little…."

"Bitchy?" I supplied and she giggled, signaling to the bartender over my shoulder and handing me a fresh drink.

"I was gonna go with *intense*, but okay. Do you live with her or something?"

I may have been out of the game for a while, but I could recognize a fishing expedition when I saw one. "As a matter of fact, I do."

The glitter in her eyes immediately dulled and I tossed a few bills on the bar, figuring that it was high time I collected Nora anyway.

Turning to leave, I gave her my best smile. "I should probably be going to get her. She likes her space, but her cancer is advancing and she'll need her meds soon."

I didn't stick around to see the effect of my words, but I could feel them in the noticeable shift in the atmosphere as I left. I'd given up my personal life to help my mom, so it wasn't the first time, nor would it be the last, that a woman had turned from attraction to judgement to chastisement and, eventually, pity upon finding out that I was less thirty-something loser and more ... I don't even know what. Martyr? Saint? Glutton for punishment?

I didn't give a shit about any part of it. As Nora herself loved to say, *it's all pretty unsatisfactory.*

The cold slapped my face the moment I stepped outside; and the bustle of the streets, the smell of roasting chestnuts, and the flurries of late December snow engulfed me. That was one thing I'd always truly loved about the city. I could be utterly and truly alone in the midst of the chaos. Absorbed by it immediately and instantly forgotten.

Maison Boutique was only a few doors down from Whiskey Charlotte's, its warmth an instant relief to the frigid evening. It looked like Christmas threw up over every square inch of it as "Let it Snow" blared from the speakers.

I picked through the tables of frames and jewelry and cookbooks and assorted other gift-worthy *tchotchkes* — my eyes scanning for violently red hair, a matching handbag, and a fur coat.

Nora insisted on continuing to wear her mink, despite the censorious glances she got on the streets as people wondered whether or not it was real. I warned her that she was going to be dodging a bucket of red paint one day and she scoffed in the truly disgusted and simultaneously superior way that only Nora could.

"Let them. It won't bring the little bastard back, will it now?"

My mother, ladies and gentlemen. She'd never been a Betty Crocker type. More the *let's-order-take-out-while-I-have-a-high-ball* type.

I made it to the checkout counter and turned back to eye the store one more time, my heart sinking a bit. The fact that I hadn't seen her did not bode well.

Turning back to the cashier, the wide-eyed look of horror plastered across her face helped my heart complete its downward trajectory until it settled in the bottom of my stomach.

"Shit, Danny, shit — I'm so sorry! She was right here and then about twenty people came up to the counter at once! It's three days before Christmas, this place is a zoo, I should never have told you I could keep an eye on her, I'm so so sorry!"

I forced a smile, despite the fact that I could instantly feel the throbbing of my blood passing through every one of my veins in time to "Have a Holly Jolly Christmas."

At this rate, the stress of taking care of Nora was going to do me in and she'd end up outliving me — fueled by spite, corticosteroids, and vermouth.

"Trish, it's fine. I get it. Where did you see her last?"

Her arm shot up as she frantically pointed to a display of Christmas trees twinkling with every conceivable variation of string lights known to man. "She was right over there looking at ornaments. I swear, it couldn't have been more than ten minutes ago."

I suppressed a sigh and headed that way. There was no way she was over there, I'd have been able to see the glow of her hair from here, but I checked anyway. Sure enough, no Nora. The trees were just inside the doors leading out to 52nd, it would have been all too easy for her to simply slip out without anyone noticing.

She had a minimum ten-minute head start and two hundred in cash on her. She could be *en route* to Connecticut by now, for all I knew.

Shoving the doors open, I stepped back out into the biting cold and looked around as if some divine intervention would tell me which way she'd gone, a slow fury beginning to burn inside me — but not at Trish, and not at Nora.

At me.

This wasn't the first time my mother had gone missing on me. About three weeks ago we'd been in the bodega down the street from her apartment — well, *our* apartment now. I was paying for our salads and she just disappeared into thin air. I'd found her just outside, but my heart had been in my throat.

"You scared me, what are you doing out here?"

She'd just continued to stare out at the street as if she hadn't heard me, watching the cars inch by in the ever-present NYC gridlock and the hair had stood up on the back of my neck.

"Nora?"

Nothing.

"Mom?"

Her head turned toward me and for a second, just a split second, no one was there. It was like she was looking through me. Then, as quickly as I'd seen it, the confusion melted away and her crystal-blue eyes flashed.

"Yes, Daniel?"

Her tone was supercilious, as if I'd interrupted her bridge game.

"What are you doing out here?"

There it was again. The flash of temper.

"Do I need to fill out a formal permit request with the city to stand on the sidewalk nowadays?"

I rolled my eyes and we made our way back to the apartment, our salads in hand, reassured by the return of her typical cheery demeanor. The nagging feeling that something was wrong wouldn't leave me, though.

I began wondering if there was more to the times that she'd pick up the phone and then put it back down without calling anyone, or the times she'd leave the front door wide open after coming home. She needed to sleep more these days, too.

I started keeping a slightly closer eye on her.

I'd tip clerks I knew around the city to text me if they saw her out without me, or to keep an eye on her when she shopped so she wouldn't know I was hovering. She really and truly hated hovering.

I should have just gone with my gut tonight and

pretended I wanted to look around for gifts too, but she'd made a big production of needing "two seconds of peace, god damn it" and I'd let her walk out of that overpriced hipster bar alone once she finished her late lunch and accompanying cocktail.

I should have known that tonight would have been a clusterfuck for Trish with the holiday chaos and all the *fa la la* bullshit. I'd call her later and apologize.

For now, I needed to find Nora. It was getting dark quick and I hadn't been lying when I'd told the girl in Charlotte's that she needed her medication. She had a nice little regimen waiting for her which she really needed to take unless she wanted to find herself potentially seizing, vomiting, or enduring a pounding headache wherever she was right now.

Fortunately, the building next door had a doorman and my mom was nothing if not completely conspicuous.

Walking over, I kept my eyes on the bustling pedestrians so I wouldn't accidentally miss her and stopped just at his side. "Hey, sorry to bother you, but did you happen to see a little old lady with bright red hair and a white fur coat come by here?"

The guy looked over at me in surprise and hope sprang hot in my chest. "Who's she to ya?"

I fought the urge to answer him through clenched teeth. "My mother. She's not well, she can't be wandering around out here."

His eyes stayed narrowed as he assessed me, but he seemed to accept my answer, "She walked back and forth in front of me a couple times. Seemed lost, so I asks her, 'Hey — what do need, ma'am? Can I call you a Yellow Cab or something?' She eyed me and told me to crawl up my own ass and die. Said it really uppity, too, like she was the freakin' queen of New York. She kept walking that way."

I slipped him a ten for the sheer fact that he'd had to speak to her in the first place and went the direction he'd jerked his head, hopeful that she hadn't gotten into a taxi. Yet, at least.

Pulling my coat collar up a bit to shield my ears from the chill, I was grateful that the time I spent between working from home and taking care of Nora left me way overdue for a haircut. It was well over my ears at this point, which was probably the only thing that would stand between me and frostbite if I had to trudge all over town looking for her.

Between the oncologist, the general doc, the neurologist, the naturopath she made me take her to on the Upper East Side for B12 shots and all of the imaging, blood work and infusion center visits, it was a wonder I even shaved anymore.

Two girls leaning against a newsstand for a quick smoke hadn't seen her. Neither had the street meat guy. The next doorman recognized her description though, because she'd asked him how to get to The Ritz.

"I told her she'd need a cab since the snow was really starting to kick up and The Park was a good twenty-minute walk from here, but she grumbled something about plebeians?"

Another ten left my possession.

C'mon, Nora, I grumbled in my own head as I stuffed my hands back into my pockets and walked on. *Are you seriously trying to go The Ritz right now? What — do you think it's time for afternoon tea?*

With a sick jolt I realized that she might.

A couple more blocks and I was about to call the cops when a flash of red caught the corner of my eye down an alley to my left. I whipped my head around, zeroed in on the source and took off at a sprint.

She was sitting on the ground next to the reeking dumpster, almost a week worth of Chinese rotting away beside her, as she looked through her bag like this was the most natural place on earth for her to be. Her coat was wet and filthy from the alley and her hair was disheveled.

"Nora, what the hell?"

Her head snapped up, "Don't you take that tone with me, you urchin. I won't allow that kind of talk — not at me. Understand?"

I squatted down to look her in the eye and saw that the confusion was back, but not like last time. There was still spunk there, her usual feistiness, but something was very, very off. It was as if my mother was sleep walking.

My tone softened considerably. "Hey — we gotta get out of here. It's snowing."

As if my pointing out something as obvious as the weather around us was the key to unlocking whatever state had overcome her, she suddenly looked around as if seeing her surroundings for the first time and then turned back to me.

Now, there was something else in her eyes. Something I'd never seen there in my entire life.

Fear.

Holding out my hand, she reached her gloved one out and took it so I could help her gently to her feet, and we made our way out of the alley. I hailed a cab immediately, all thoughts centering around getting her warm and dry.

She went with me without argument. That was almost the most heartbreaking part of the whole damn thing.

"I think I'm losing my mind, Daniel."

Until she said that.

I loaded her into the car and pushed both of the heat vents at her the minute we drove off toward home, the TV in the back immediately launching into its in-ride programming. I completely tuned it out, my eyes fixed on the woman who'd raised me.

I'd never seen her look so … frail. This was the woman who'd made the schoolyard bully cry after she'd marched onto the playground and pulled him off of me — telling him that there was a place in Jersey for evil children where they only served cockroaches for dinner and the wardens beat them and the children could never go home again.

We were six.

She'd harangued him until his mother showed up and then Nora had made *her* cry, too. This woman was invincible, nothing and no one screwed with her.

My mind started cycling through blips of memories like a montage in one of the ridiculous Lifetime movies she made me watch all the time.

Nora making cookies from pre-made grocery store dough and almost burning the apartment down when she forgot to turn the stove off in all of the excitement of her domestic success.

Nora casually sipping her drink and telling me my father drowned in the Hudson after a drunken bender when I was two. I was 9 at the time.

Nora sleeping on my floor if I had a fever so she could check me compulsively through the night.

Nora telling my ex (a respected junior partner in a small accounting firm) that she'd call her office and ask for the senior partner every single day pretending to be my ex's drunken mother offering sex favors for her daughter's career advancement if my ex dared ask for spousal support that she didn't need in the divorce. ("Darling, I've got the time and I've got the balls. Try me.")

Nora going for a cocktail and making a toast after being told that her tumor was back and that it was not only inoperable but also terminal. ("A drink to my friend Glio B. Lastoma — we're off to hell together.")

We pulled up in front of our building and I walked around the cab to try to help her inside, upon which she flippantly shook me off and marched toward the door on her own.

She shuffled up the stairs and through the front door ahead of me and I watched powerlessly as she set her purse down on the side table, shrugged slowly out of her ruined coat and then gingerly pulled her signature red hair off of her head to place it on the wig stand. The hair beneath it was short and white and not quite fully back from the chemo that had proven so very disappointingly ineffective.

She looked small and old and something inside of me broke. She was a giant pain in the ass, but I was losing her. I was losing my mom.

"Can I get you something?" I asked, knowing I couldn't show her the sympathy or affection I wanted to. She'd accuse me of thinking her weak. Then she'd insist that *I* was the weak one.

"There's nothing in this world or the next that makes the toil of this living hell worth a good god damn, Daniel."

I put my hands in my pockets and met her gaze as she turned to look at me, her eyes as blue and clear and sharp as ever.

"Oh, I don't know about that Mom." I said, a light smile on my face despite the growing heaviness in my heart. "You've still got coffee and whiskey sours. There's pecan sandies in the cabinet." I paused before plowing on, needing her to know she wasn't alone in all of this. "You've got me."

She turned on her heel and scoffed, heading toward her bedroom. "That may be," Nora said, "but it's all pretty unsatisfactory."

"Missing Nora"

J J DOLMAGE is a freelance writer and hairstylist, working in Arizona, in the United States. She's a champion-level thrift shopper with a zeal for a deal; likes cuddling with her golden retriever; and ascribes to the philosophy that no matter what, everything will turn out alright as long as we have donuts. "Missing Nora" is her first published story.

She says: "My father was the quintessential Irish character and, while quite unlike the character of Nora in attitude (I actually borrowed a bit from my grandmother to create her special brand of sass), he embodied that irrepressible spirit that made everyone think he was invincible. When he passed, and we discovered that he wasn't, the process of disbelief and grief mixed with admiration stood out as a singular one — and this story was born."

Thursday Afternoon

I WAS LEANING against the bar in a speakeasy on 52nd street, waiting for Nora to finish her Christmas shopping, when a girl got up from the table where she had been sitting with three other people and came over to me. The first thing that struck me was her scent — no, her *smell*. It was a harsh cocktail of cigarette smoke and cinnamon that stung the back of my throat. It clouded around her, lingering on her fingertips as they curled around my hand in a lazy handshake, and dancing along her tongue as she introduced herself simply as Grey. The smile that followed was forced, just the empty casing of what was maybe a genuine, warm, grin many moons ago. It remained etched on her face until I took it as my cue to speak.

"Elizabeth," I replied, setting my empty glass down. "Can I help you?"

She blinked for a moment, peering into my face as if I had just told her I was the queen of planet Mars. Her eyes were unfocused, practically looking straight through me. Once she was satisfied, she nodded and leaned against the bar beside me.

"So, you're English?" she asked, ignoring my question. "I love England."

"You've been?"

"God, no," she shook her head, resting her elbows on the bar.

Tipsy conversation with strangers wasn't unusual, yet here I was trying to determine if her eyes were green or hazel. Something made me want to ask her questions. She drew the curiosity out of me. I studied her as she ordered a drink, a concoction of poisons that I imagined would taste much like acid mixed with paint stripper.

"Can I help you?" I repeated.

"No," the woman replied, as she tried to make eye contact with the bartender, "but I could help you."

Doubtful was the reply that hung on my lips. *Tell me more* was not far behind it. *Leave me alone* was suddenly nesting at the bottom of the list.

"How so?" I asked, settling on the most neutral response I could muster.

She caught the bartender's attention and upon his return began reciting her order again, twirling one of her black ringlets around her ring-clad finger as she spoke. It had fallen from her updo but she didn't bother fixing it back into place. When the server started to move away, she followed, trailing her hand along the bar as she continued to instruct him on measures and volumes. I had never seen anybody be so precise and particular with their order here; I wouldn't dare ask for anything more complicated than a cheap glass of moonshine.

I took this time to glance over to the trio of guests at her table. The oldest of the three was a silver-haired gentleman, with a strong Roman nose and an immaculately-tailored suit. The suit in all its pinstriped glory was fully visible as he stood, gesturing wildly as he entertained the people at the next table. He used two chairs as props, much to the amusement of his observers. He was a storyteller, it seemed, and an exceptional one at that.

The seat facing me was occupied by a man no younger than me, maybe twenty-four or so. He was sallow and frowning and wearing a shirt stained with either jam or blood. His eyes were glazed over, and if it wasn't for the fact the wrinkles in his shirt shifted across his wiry frame every time he breathed, I might have wondered if he was dead.

The final person was turned away from me. All I could see was a shock of auburn hair that curved in rich red locks around his — or her — neck. They wore a dazzling gold ring on their left hand that caught the light as they lifted their glass, and I was transfixed when they twisted around to look directly at me and Grey. They were the most striking person I had ever seen, completely androgynous and totally magnetising….

Before I knew what was happening, Grey had taken my hand and led me away.

The rain was bitter against my skin. It was a sunny autumn morning when Nora and I had left but now my mustard yellow dress was not holding up on this drizzly Thursday afternoon. I wished I had brought a coat, or picked up an umbrella, or just gone shopping with Nora and avoided this whole situation in the first place. I wondered if she would panic when she couldn't find me, or if she would assume I had gone home. The thought of her worrying about me was heartbreaking enough, but the idea of her leaving me behind with this strange woman and her mismatched band of acquaintances….

Grey yanked me into an alley, a sharp movement that jarred my shoulder. As she walked ahead I noticed a maze of intricate patterns, almost like scarring, that curved with her bones. They danced over her undulating shoulder blades as she wrenched open a wooden door at the foot of the alleyway. All I could focus on as she ushered me inside was how long Nora would sit at our kitchen table waiting for me if I disappeared. Maybe a day. Then she would storm out of there and find me herself. Or at least, she would try.

Once we were inside, Grey flicked a switch and the long passageway before me illuminated. There was a staircase at the end of it, narrow and tumbling down into another dimly-lit room below. Grey almost crashed into me as I hesitated on the top step. She must have been looking somewhere else. My grip on the splintering banister just about saved us both.

"You can leave any time," she stated, eyes lifting from her hands. "You came here voluntarily. I'll escort you back to that ghastly bar, if you so wish."

I shook my head and embraced the curiosity that was clouding my mind. Downstairs I was met by the older gentleman from the bar and his two accomplices. I feared the confusion was evident on my face.

"We took a shortcut," the older man greeted me with a smile.

"A shortcut?" I pressed, "Where exactly are we?"

Grey pondered for a second before answering in a careful tone. "A hideout."

"A hideout?"

"Must you repeat everything?" the younger man interjected.

"Must you be so rude?" Grey snapped. "Or is that just part of your nature?" Her eyes were fixed on me. In the short time I had known Grey I had picked up on her habit of looking elsewhere. It was as though her mind was too quick for her mouth, always scoping out the next adventure. My gaze shot over to the redhead, who until this point had said nothing. I had forgotten how cold I was until I looked into their eyes. The irises were pure gold, and their vibrancy reminded me of the flurrying embers that spat from the old hearth in my messy living room. My hands toyed with the rain-sodden hem of my dress. Maybe this was more than the result of a tipsy conversation on a Thursday afternoon.

"So," said the redhead, "the purpose of this trip is still unknown to you, yes?"

"Oh, she goes by Elizabeth," Grey chimed in before I

could answer.

"Wait," I piped up, feeling my blood shudder in my arteries. "My name. You said I *go by* Elizabeth. What do you mean?"

"We've been learning about you for a little while now," the redhead elaborated. "We then needed to locate you. Elizabeth is your middle name, correct?"

I didn't reply. I felt nauseated, like my body was coated in a cold sweat inside and out, and all I could think about was how I'd opted to sit in a smoky old speakeasy alone instead of helping Nora pick out the perfect tie for her brother's Christmas gift. I just wanted to wake up in bed, safe from this bizarre dream. I wouldn't have cared if I'd drifted back into consciousness right that second on the speakeasy floor, decorated with a black eye after getting caught up in a fight between strangers. Instead, I stood facing a panel who all somehow knew that Elizabeth wasn't my first name. I nodded, a quick gesture that made my head feel heavier than marble.

"Your full name is Madeleine Elizabeth Kingfisher. Correct?"

"I'd like to go home," I told them, keeping my voice measured. "I can find my way back, I just need to leave. Whatever this is, I don't want any part of it."

"Elizabeth," Grey sighed, "I said you could leave."

"Right," I huffed. "Off I go, then."

I was halfway up the staircase when Grey asked, "But aren't you curious?"

I hated to admit it but I was desperate to know how they knew my name and where to find me. As keen as I was to get back to Nora, I knew my mind would never settle if I left right now. I bit the bullet.

"You have sixty seconds to explain," I fired back in a voice that sounded twice as confident as I had ever felt in my life. "Clock's ticking."

The younger man laughed, rocking back on his chair precariously. Grey turned and headed towards an old bookcase at the base of the stairs. The redhead's eyes honed in on her feline movements, watching as Grey lifted herself on top of it and folded her legs under herself like a child.

"Oh, I want a good seat for this," Grey quipped, cupping her chin in her hands and resting her elbows against her knees. "You heard young Elizabeth. Clock's ticking."

I didn't know what to expect. Part of me wanted them to announce that this was a surprise party six weeks before my birthday. That Nora was behind the whole thing — her beaming face would've been the most welcome sight in the world at that moment. Another part of me was waiting for them to tell me they were from the secret service and that I was about to be whisked away to some distant land for my own safety. An even tinier part of me thought this might be a practical joke on behalf of someone who didn't like me — there were plenty of suspects in our neighbourhood who sneered at me and Nora as we passed them on the street. However, I was skeptical that our ninety-year-old next door neighbour John would be determined enough to plan a heist so meticulous. I drummed my fingers against the banister anxiously.

"My name is Death. I'm looking for an apprentice."

"This has to be a joke," I scoffed. "Nobody's name is Death. I mean, I'm not fond of my own name, but I'd choose it any day over that."

"Are you in shock? This is the first time you've laughed all afternoon," Grey noted. "Anyway, Madeleine is a beautiful name. You should use it."

"It's not a joke," the redhead — Death — informed me, ignoring Grey. "Death is a name that was given to me centuries ago. Now it is growing tired of me. It needs a replacement, and it has chosen you."

"Well, I'm not an apprentice," I explained. "I'm a librarian."

"Death does not choose lightly," they said, ochre eyes gleaming. "The name embodies only those it finds worthy. It's an honour to be considered."

Several thoughts hit me at once. One was how much I hated spending my days in that stuffy library. Another was how desperately I wanted to be at home listening to Nora talk excitedly about her day. The final thought was: *Did I just say yes?*

"Excellent," Death responded.

"What does this entail? Will I be sworn in by blood for the rest of eternity? If so, I'd like to change my mind. Unless that's not allowed, then I suppose I don't have a choice in the matter, do I?"

"Definitely shock," Grey decided, leaping down like a tabby. "Death embodies those it deems worthy of carrying its name. As an apprentice, you only swear in for the trial. Take the first three names on the list, then we'll talk."

"Do I … kill people?"

"At least you were told," the young man sneered. "I only applied for a job in administration. Besides, a year here feels like a decade."

"It feels like a century for us with all of your complaining," Grey retorted before turning her attention to me. "Every death is predetermined. All you need to do is guide them into the afterlife and make sure they don't get lost along the way. As an apprentice you'll live a mostly normal life, like a day job until Death retires from its current entity."

"Like a helping hand?"

"Precisely. I lead them to the Index where Malachi processes their information." Grey then gestured to the sleeping gentleman. "And the lovely Mr Whittaker here makes them feel at home. Nothing has to be scary."

"Elizabeth," Death interjected, "your word is your bond."

"I'll try it," I decided, taking Death's outstretched hand.

The air that rushed over me was like ice in my veins. It seared every inch of me, buckling my legs and burning my eyes like they'd been submerged in a vat of chlorine. I couldn't feel anything beneath me, just my own frostbitten body spiraling against a void. *I'm blind*, my mind screamed. I thought of Nora's face and how I might not see it again — her gap-toothed smile, her hazel doe eyes, her masses of chestnut curls, her freckled nose. *I'm blind.*

Suddenly I could see everything like it was freshly painted. Clear, bright, and a little too focused. I staggered to my feet, eyes brimming with tears and knees grazed. Wordlessly, Grey handed me a mirror. My eyes were bloodshot and weeping but the irises were deep ochre.

"Nobody can see it apart from us," she said. "They'll still look blue."

"Right," I responded, still puzzled. "So, why —"

"Why could you see Death's eyes?" Malachi cut me off, "Because you were selected as the apprentice. I don't know why, though. You're not particularly astute."

"They help draw you to the client," Death explained. "Shall we begin?"

"Okay," I said, feeling the anxiety bubbling in my stomach.

"The first name on our list," Death said, "is Nora Jane Campbell."

I don't remember how I got to the speakeasy. I remember shrieking and falling and biting down as hard as I could on Grey's hand as she tried to lift me. When I first froze, Malachi took great delight in reminding me that this was my trial and that I had sworn to do this. But when I found myself spitting up blood from screaming until my throat was raw, he fell silent. And then I was there, standing in the middle of a crowded bar feeling like my entire world had been chewed up and spat into my face.

"We're essentially invisible when we're working," Death informed me. "Your task is simple: approach the client and touch their hand — you'll know when it's time." I didn't bother replying. I didn't care enough about Death's instructions to acknowledge them. I didn't know how I was going to manage this. I didn't want anything other than to be sat at my kitchen table listening to the radio on a rainy Christmas Eve. That stung the most. She loved Christmas more than anything. And now she wouldn't get another. My heart found a new home in my mouth, buzzing behind my teeth like a vengeful wasp. I forced it down.

She was tipsily talking to the bartender, a vision of unruly curls, olive skin, and an untouched drink. I took in the way her nose crinkled and the flecks of green in her irises. She was kind and charismatic and everything good in the world. And totally unaware of what was about to happen. For Nora this was just another Thursday afternoon. She told him about her job at the hospital, our house with a real apple tree in the garden, the burgundy tie she had bought, how eager she was for Christmas — and finally, me.

"I think my darling might be the loveliest thing in this world," she mused.

"Better than a real beer? Ice cold on a hot day?"

"Most definitely," Nora hummed. "No, I don't think. I *know*. Love is what keeps this world on its axis. It keeps us warm and safe and balanced. It's the most wonderful sensation."

"There's a lot more to life than love."

I reached out, placing my hand over hers like I had done so many times before. She had a dreamy look in her eyes, one that made my heart ache in a way I'd never experienced before. Holding back the acid in my throat, I kept a fraction of an inch between us. Then, eyes closed, I lowered my hand to hers.

"That may be," Nora said, "but it's all pretty unsatisfactory."

"Thursday Afternoon"

KERRI ASHES recently graduated university in Liverpool, England, with a degree in Linguistics. When not studying or writing, she's a barista, pulling shots. Her work has been published in the *Young Writers Poetry Anthology* and she was shortlisted for the Lancaster Writing Awards.

She says: "The pieces fell into place fairly quickly, with the final story coming together in a day. I focused on making Nora and Elizabeth's relationship as authentic as possible; Elizabeth's first thought at every turn is Nora, so I wanted readers to understand why she cares so much about her. I really enjoyed writing about Elizabeth as she's such a conflicted character — her curiosity and impulsivity fuel the story, but they also cause her the most regret in the end."

Patrick Roycroft

The Unsatisfactory Man

I WAS LEANING against the bar in a speakeasy on 52nd street, waiting for Nora to finish her Christmas shopping, when a girl got up from the table where she had been sitting with three other people and came over to me.

"Feeling lonely?" she asked.

At my best I often consider myself to be a dude, a player, a magnet for women of discernment and intelligence. Spend some time with me, see me in my element, and you'll realise I'm a special kind of guy. On that particular day I was not in my element. Far from it, I was down in the basement, hiding and licking some old wounds. So why was a gorgeous chihuahua wondering if I was lonely? Was she hooking me?

"Alone for now, not sure that means I'm lonely. My little *liebeschnauzer* is away spending my money."

"Your *liebeschnauzer*? So you call your lady your *love snouter*?"

"Love *terrier*, that's what I call her because she's feisty, she's built that way, it's a term of endearment."

"I see, and she's spending your money is she, honey? Do you feel a little special knowing that it's your money that she depends on?"

She looked at me with such a clear gaze with her bright blue eyes. She stirred up a pack of emotions that I struggled to identify, but there was one feeling that I could identify because it was all too familiar. The feeling that she could read me better than I could read her, and better than I could read myself.

"When I earn it I like to see it spent on people I care for."

"Does it make you feel good because it's a good thing to give, or does it just feel good because it makes you feel powerful?"

I could see her studying me, appraising my every expression and choice of words with cool skill and a clear determination to understand me. Interested in me. Interested in my feelings. Was her interest real or was she really just interested in my money? Was she even real?

"If it's a power trip, does it also give you a little tingle of terror, like she might be using you? She might just be taking you for a ride, just to get what she wants."

I struggled to get a grip on this one. Her questions had started to feel intrusive. What kind of understanding of me was she building and why? Suspicions stirred in me, so I threw her a curve-ball to buy a little time.

"Sure, she's on the take, but I like that."

"She's on the take and you actually like that?"

"I like that! It's honest, means she's human just like the rest of us fleshpots, don't you think?"

"You're a man who likes a smokescreen, a man who likes to throw a little chaos into the works, are you?"

I looked away from her and at my drink. She moved closer, and placed her handbag on the bar.

"I earn enough. I like to see her spending it."

"Earn enough, huh? That supposed to impress me? Money means nothing to me. If a man like you is a good man, then you can keep any woman satisfied without money being involved at all."

This cut through my suspicions about her being a working girl, human or otherwise, looking for business. I stopped studying my whiskey and tried again to focus on her. Was she a special kind of girl who could see the real me? Could she see that special me that I can be when I get beyond the hassle of daily dog-eat-dog life? Could she feel that I can also be a loser, a swine, a repulsive force to any intelligent life? A guy like me has to be a bit careful.

"I can be a good man, and I can also be a swine."

"Like all men of the flesh then, that's nothing special."

"Well, I happen to think I am a little special, and I'm thinking you are, too."

She started humming. The tune was vaguely familiar but I just couldn't place it. I admit I was finding her more and more attractive, more than a little edgy, and she was engaging with parts of me I thought were long lost.

She moved closer and said, "You certainly are intriguing. You been staring at that whiskey for half an hour and you haven't touched it. Is it special, too? Too good to drink?"

"I'm not a well man … I can't drink."

"You can't drink? So you buy one just to admire, or just to fit in around here?"

"To test myself. That's why I come here. I love to drink. I love to drink so much that I can't drink. That right there is my problem, my special problem."

"I love to drink, too," she said. She moved closer again, real close, and placing her hand on mine she said, "Lets drink together. I drink from the never-ending fountain called love! Do you want to drink from that fountain, too? Let's drink from the fountain of love!"

"Hell, yeah. Whatever's happening here, I'm in! Here's to love!" I said, and then downed my whiskey in one. The centre of gravity of my life shifted right there. Things were never going to be the same again. I just hadn't realised it yet.

"I love you!" She said and hugged me. "I am Crystal Clear, and I am sent here to save your soul. I love you, and the Lord loves you…."

Crystal reached into her handbag and brought out a Bible and handed it to me, singing a vaguely familiar hymn to that vaguely familiar tune she'd been humming. Her voice was pitch perfect but bombastic. With the singing over she put her arms around me and looking right into my eyes she said, "Do you want to be *saved*, brother?"

"Ahh, schnapps! You tricked me! When you first came over I guessed you must be made. Nothing as beautiful as you could've just evolved by chance in my life! First I thought you were a hooker-bot, then you asked if I wanted a drink and started on about love! You tricked me! You made me think you were the girl of my dreams! You aren't a girl at all, are you — you're one of those holier-than-thou bible-bots sent here to convert me to —"

"I'm an Evangelica-bot, brother, built and programmed by Christ's Daughters of the Baptist Revolution. I didn't make you think anything, honey, you do all your thinking yourself, and that's your problem. You assumed I wanted you to drink whisky. I wanted you to drink the love of The Lord. That's what you really need. Right now you are lost, my brother."

"Same again?" asked Sid the Same Again Squid from behind the bar. The Same Again Squid is a good decent straightforward bot that does just what it claims, sitting in the middle of the bar it picks up empties with its tentacles and, having detected what you've been drinking via its sensitive suckers, it asks if you'd like another.

Sid's Bar is one of those new bars staffed entirely by bots. Sid the Squid, along with wisecracking skunks, rats with listening skills, and hog's with top-notch humour, are all top-end entertainment bots endowed with state of the art facial expressions, language skills, and voice tones.

"Sid, that would be mighty fine. You're a fine fellow," I replied, but as I did so a skunk, who had been perched on the bar the whole time, said "Not so fast, Sid."

The skunk scurried towards me and placed his paw on my hand.

"Sir, you are under arrest. I am Pepe. I am a bar-bot and a government compliance-bot," he said. He turned to

Crystal.

"Like you, sister, I am here to help these struggling flesh-bods. However, I am not programmed to believe any of your doctrines. I am legally-entitled to serve drinks. I am also legally-mandated to report any and all breaches of any Prohibition and Treatment Orders that occur on these premises."

Pepe then turned to me and said, "My facial recognition is updated constantly, and you, sir, are Nicholas, commonly known as Charles comma Nick. You are currently subject to Prohibition and Treatment Order number seven-zero-two-two-eight-four-four-seven from City Court Central."

My thoughts scampered around and settled on a rather dim-witted response. "Ahhhh, *schnapps* — and a double schnapps and salty fecker fishes!"

Crystal turned to Pepe and said, "Spare this poor sinner, he is being saved!"

I squared up to Pepe and added, "Yeah, spare me, Pepsy, give this sinner a break. They got you working two jobs, serving folks their drinks and then grounding them, that's government for you. You should complain, it's a conflict of interest for you, my little furry friend."

Without even an imitation smile or humanising blink the skunk replied, "Sir, you are forbidden from consuming alcohol. You have just consumed two standard measures of whiskey. You are also on a programme to improve your relationship management skills. You are clearly flirting with this Evangelica-bot under the mistaken assumption that she is a sexually-available human female. You are therefore in breach of three priority areas of your Treatment Order."

"Three? You only mentioned the two."

"No. Three. Your programme includes a mandatory module on developing emotional intelligence. Flirting while your partner is shopping also counts against you as a failure to practice emotional intelligence and self-regulation. The fact that you clearly failed to notice that you were relating to a bot — not a human — demonstrates continued neglect of your emotional intelligence skills. Someone practising emotionally-sensitive conversation would have noticed that Crystal was not displaying normal human emotional needs. You were solely focused on yourself and your needs. Crystal was just an object to you, a device through which to project and satisfy yourself."

"You don't say!"

"I do say," said the skunk.

He jumped onto my arm and scampered up, grabbing my ears with his paws as he brought his furry face right into mine. Nose to nose we stared into one another's eyes, neither of us blinking.

"Get your paws off me, Pepsy, you're not showing such good social skills yourself right now, you're violating my personal space," I told him while practising just enough of the basic emotional regulation skills to prevent me from getting physical with the skunk. A slight amount of tension did manifest in my voice.

"I detect that you are a little angry with me, Mr. Charles," replied Pepe with an annoying conciliatory tone. "However, I am mandated to use reasonable force to restrain you while I report your misdemeanours immediately to your personal treatment-bot. I have already done so."

I contemplated making a run for it, though what that 'it' could be I hadn't yet figured out. While I struggled to string some thoughts together to make a plan, the skunk-bot struck. Without warning, but with steely android speed and stealth, it turned around, raised its tail, and released a cloud of pungent taser-gas from its hind quarters, which left me juddering and jabbering and falling to the floor.

Crystal leant forward and prayed over me, then she offered to share my sins.

As the juddering stopped, I was left with a toxic fog of feelings. Angry, humiliated, and confused I wondered whether all the patrons at Sid's bar were in fact bots programmed by various government departments, police departments, or churches.

Thoughts floundered through the fog: *It's all a set up! Nora dropped me here on the way to the shops on purpose to test me! I'm a sucker! To fall for a bible-bot. To be deluded enough to think she was real and wanted me. To get busted and lectured on what it means to be a good man — by a skunk-bot no less!*

Then I managed to speak. The taser-gas was affecting me, so my words sounded as if they were coming from a blubber-mouthed sloth, but they were words from the human heart.

"To cwote de late grape Stefen Awking: *wiv out impafection weeee woood not egg-zist*. Dis is jus a mix up, a slip up and a spot of bovver. May-beee I bended de rules of da court but I haven't bwoken dem … only a little … I spilled most of the dwink…."

"Save it for the judge, Nicholas, known as Nick," said Pepe, peering down at me from his perch on a bar stool. "I just checked that quote on multiple databases. The quotation from Professor Hawking is actually *without imperfection neither you nor I would exist*. The reasoning implicit in the use of this quotation I understand. My Psych programming suggests your motives for drinking were clear, crystal clear. You did not spill any significant quantity of your drink."

At that point I tried to sit up, but I passed out.

When I came around Nora had arrived. The skunk had put me in cuffs while I had been unconscious and was still sitting on a bar stool telling Nora the whole story.

A rat-bot was perched on my chest keeping an eye on me.

"Are you all right, sir?"

"I just got bible-bashed, badgered, and blasted with taser-gas, so what do you think?" The rat snorted and put its nose right in my ear and whispered.

"Sir, I would hazard the opinion that you're feeling low.

I express sympathy for your suffering."

The rat-bot pulled its nose back out of my ear and its face assumed the shape of sympathetic pity.

"I thought being badgered by a skunk was bad, but you know your life can't get lower when you're pitied by a rat." And then, even though I knew the rat wasn't alive, wasn't really feeling sympathy just expressing it as a programmed response, I opened my heart and cried out to it.

"I got feisty bastard parts in here! I got mean scared smelly meaty sides to me! How can I get outa this one? How can any of you bots really understand? How can you know what it's like to be human? I got a nasty, messy mind, OK, but a human mind evolved over millions of years to cope with a nasty, messy world. I wasn't designed by a genius and built in a nice clean factory! You don't fart, you don't *need* anyone or anything … you don't eat or screw or feel shit about yourselves … you don't even have real assholes to keep clean!"

Nora walked towards me and looked at me with a startlingly similar expression to that still being maintained by my rodent sympathiser.

"Ok, I had a drink, *one lousy drink* which I know is one drink too many … and, ok, I talked to a pretty woman …well, I thought she was a woman … but I hadn't been unfaithful … hadn't even stole a kiss, let alone any slips and slaps … just some chit chat is all…."

"That may be," Nora said, "but it's all pretty unsatisfactory."

"The Unsatisfactory Man"

PATRICK ROYCROFT is a clinical psychologist in Newcastle, England. He writes with his right hand, which may or may not be because it's the hand that squeezed the hand that boxing legend Muhammad Ali used to conquer his world, and the hand that Booker T Jones uses to play his cracking soul music. "The Unsatisfactory Man" is his first published story.

He says: "I loved this competition — a real brain teaser. I have not read *The Thin Man*, but the lines created a strong impression and an immediate desire to know what happens to the characters, so I quickly jotted this story down. I enjoyed rewriting it more slowly, and found that it tickled me, so I hope it tickles you."

Female Jockeys

I WAS LEANING against the bar in a speakeasy on 52nd street, waiting for Nora to finish her Christmas shopping, when a girl got up from the table where she had been sitting with three other people and came over to me. She slid in to the seat beside me and the ring she was wearing caught itself on the edge of my sleeve. I looked down at the gentle curve of the girl's wrist and the way she ran her fingers carelessly across my sleeve to free the ring, and thought I might die. She drew her thumb across the large green jewel that was set in the ring, pried it loose from my sleeve, and flashed her eyes up to mine.

"It's a fake, but a good one," she said. She gave me a wink like we were old pals and the embers flared beneath my cheeks. "What's a girl got to do to get a drink around here?"

The girl's moist lips were two inches from my face and a hot thought ripped through me before I wrestled it back underground. I was not a quick or snappy sort of person, but I was desperate to keep the girl's attention, so I took a chance and said,

"Have a purse full of money or the eye of a fella?"

The girl's laughter fell over us like fresh snow. She leaned back on her elbow to appraise me, and I felt the edges of my collar burning though my neck. She looked down at my meaty hands, their nails bitten to the quick, and made her judgement.

"That ain't what life's got planned for a couple a gals like us."

My eyes bounced over to Nora, who was sitting down at the end of the bar counting her coins. I took a long breath and willed her to stay put, but I knew in my heart what was coming.

My mind drifted back to earlier that afternoon. I had been halfway through my seventh cigarette when Nora had announced we were going Christmas shopping. I had figured we were off to the dry goods store on the corner, but apart from a quick stop for Lucky Strikes, we had beaten a straight path to the back door of The Jefferson speakeasy.

Nora had looked over her shoulder, eased open the door, and said,

"We'll get all our gifts *here* this year, Charlie."

My heart had sunk when she had said it because being in public with Nora was a special kind of hell.

"We should be spending our money on gifts for the family, Charlie, but since they are all dead to us, we'll spend it on bourbon instead. One shot for each one of the goddamn bastards, down the hatch."

Nora had chuckled and disappeared through the doorway. I had stood outside and braced myself for a doozy of an evening. When Nora got a hold of her bourbon, she became the world's most enthusiastic charlatan. I had known that she would take all of the poor saps at The Jefferson half way to China before they had even realized they were out the front door.

I had badly wanted to skip the whole situation, but there were two reasons I hadn't. The first being that despite hating her, I loved Nora; and the second being that she was my mother and even though I was twenty-six, I couldn't shake the feeling that I was obliged to do what she said.

So I sat at the bar of The Jefferson, drinking soda, smoking my sixteenth Lucky Strike, and steeling myself for the inevitable. You wouldn't catch me swimming in bourbon and making an ass of myself downtown.

Nora slapped her coins down and called over Slim Bobby.

"First one's for Bert," she said. Slim grabbed the bourbon without missing a beat and I realized this wasn't the first time Nora had done her Christmas shopping at The Jefferson.

Bert was Nora's Pa who, despite his own hot temper and fast hands, had expected better things from his daughter than she had ultimately delivered.

Nora belted back her bourbon in one hard swallow and slammed her cup on the bar. "Worst father I never had," she said.

Nora looked up, saw I was talking to the girl, and stood up like a squirrel who saw a nut. She smoothed the ample bodice of her one good dress, and hurried toward us.

"Charlie, honey, ain't you gonna introduce me?" she said.

The girl perked up for old Nora and offered her a hand.

"Name's Phyllis, Ma'am."

The way they shook hands was fishy. I saw Phyllis give Nora a little wink and I wondered what the hell was going on. Slim slid a drink across the bar and the moment passed.

"There you go, Phil, another Gin Ricky for my best girl," said Slim. Phyllis gave him a giggle and I thought less of her for submitting to his oily charm.

Nora knocked her empty glass against the bar. *"Second one's for Freddie,"* she said.

Freddie was the slick mink who had once encouraged Nora to make a bad decision in the middle of a hay field. The first lie Freddie had told Nora was that if she held still, it wouldn't be so bad. The second lie had been that he'd stay.

"Floppy-eared Jackal, laughed me all the way to ruin."

I touched the sides of my own oversized ears and thought about the sucker punch Freddie had landed eight months after he had gone.

Slim passed Nora her second bourbon and smiled sideways. Nora raised her eyebrows and they were thick as thieves.

Phyllis sucked the lime from her Gin Ricky and I snuck a better look at her. On second pass, she lost some of her shine. She was a touch plump and had a light fuzz over her top lip. That was all fine by me because the more that was wrong with Phyllis, the better the chance she would stay talking to me. It was not long before she caught me looking.

"What do you say, Charlie, am I just your size?"

I grabbed the inside of my lip with my teeth and tried not to breathe. I knew what could happen to a girl who showed too much interest.

Nora got jittery from all the lack of attention and tipped her glass toward Phyllis.

"Tell me, Phil, where's home?"

I knew what was coming next and I couldn't stand it. Nora and I lived in a couple of rooms above a Five-and-Dime, but that wasn't the story she was about to tell Phyllis. Whenever she started out asking someone where their home was, I knew she was about to do the horse-racing bit.

"I'm from Syracuse originally, Ma'am, what about you?"

Nora had her on the line then, and she and Phyllis were off to China.

"I'm a country girl, Phil. My Pa owned near half of Wayne County out in the Poconos and I was riding horses before I could walk."

I thought of the marginal operation north of Sioux City where Nora had spent her miserable childhood and it was almost comical.

Phyllis forgot all about me at that point. That was how it always went. I would almost have a conversation with some nice-looking girl and then old Nora would come over and start laying down some story to scare her off.

"You see, Phil, my Pa raced horses all the way from Boise to Columbus, the finest fillies in the State of Pennsylvania. A lot of folks frown on a woman in the saddle, but not my Pa. He let me ride those horses over god's great earth till I came home sore as sunshine. My brother never could swallow that I rode those horses better than he could. If they had let me race, I would have been state champion."

I sipped my soda and wondered how she could stand herself. I knew who my people were, and I would sell my own eyes if any forward-thinking Pennsylvanian horse barons were among them. When Nora's Pa had found out about her condition, he had told her he didn't have no daughter who whored herself out in a hay field so she had better just go ahead and get off his land and forget she ever lived there.

Nora paused her lying long enough to realize she was fresh out of bourbon. Slim poured the third shot and said, "This one's for Walter, if memory serves."

"On the money, Slim. *Best brother Abel ever had.*"

Walter was Nora's big brother who had thought himself generous for offering to take Nora in. His only condition had been that she come without the baby. Given the terms of her tenancy, Nora had decided to skip town.

Nora had turned out to be a pretty awful mother, but one thing I could say for her was that she knew what was hers. It was easier to travel with a baby on the inside, so Nora had left the farm that very night along with all of the money in Walter's cash box.

I looked over at Phyllis, who was sipping her Gin Ricky and eating up Nora with her eyes.

"I'd love to be able to ride a horse like that," she said. "I imagine it's a right thrill."

"Nothing better, Phil, than to be a female jockey."

I died inside when she said that, as if a female jockey was a genuine, actual thing. Phyllis looked at Nora like she was pure churned butter and not just a drunk old hussy who lived above a Five-and-Dime with her lame-duck daughter.

As far as I saw it, I had never had a chance. Nora had birthed me in the back room of a Chelsea tenement, and it had not been long before we had found ourselves with no way to pay the rent. Nora being Nora, she had gathered a few local floozies to alternate child-minding with working the streets. Most mornings of my childhood, I had woken up to some damp-haired beauty sleeping it off on our spare mattress.

"*Last shot's for Marion*, Slim."

Marion had been Nora's top Floozy. It was her who had given me my first taste of hellfire and I briefly considered ordering my own bourbon just for her.

One night I had woken up to Marion's rum soaked breath on my cheek and she had said, "Hey, Charlie, have you ever felt like kissing a woman?" Marion had caught my trembling lips in hers, and it was as close to Eden as I had ever been.

The next morning, Marion and Nora had blown the top off of everything and as Marion was storming out the door, she had looked straight at me and announced to Nora,

"Just so you know, sweetie, your girl Charlie is a bigger trapeze artist than you ever were."

When Marion had gone, Nora had looked at me with regret and had said,

"Charlie, those inclinations are pretty unsatisfactory. It's no way to live, believe me. The best thing you can do is to pretend to be some way else and find yourself a fella."

That was when I had started the slow process of burying myself, and it probably went a long way to explaining why I could not talk to a girl without gnawing off my own hand.

I choked a little on my soda and Phyllis gave me a quick look. I inspected my nails and realized that I had made a mess of things. Phyllis followed my gaze, saw the blood rising on the sides of my fingers, and lifted her pretty lips a titch. It reminded me of the way Marion had looked at me right before she had closed the door.

Nora got impatient for the punchline of her story so she started to run the home stretch.

"I tell ya, Phil, it's a wondrous thing to climb on the back of a horse and just let it take you off to the other side of the sunset. It's the only time I've ever felt totally alive."

"But why did you stop, Ma'am?"

Nora looked up and caught my eye in the reflection of the hazy mirror behind the bar. "I got careless, Phil. Had a big fall off of one of those animals and was too injured to get back in the saddle."

A hot tear inched down Nora's cheek as she drained the last drops of Bourbon from her glass. I might have felt sorry for her, had I not heard the story a hundred times and believed it less with each telling.

Phyllis and Slim turned toward me and from the way they were mugging, I knew they could see right through my skin and in to the beating heart of the matter. Nora was crying in her bourbon and you did not have to look too far to see who's fault that all was.

Everyone got quiet and I knew they were expecting me to mop up the whole goddamn scene. My eyes burned, but you wouldn't catch me crying to a fuzzy lipped honey and some two bit soda jerk. I was so sore at Nora for the look she had given me in the mirror that I did something I've never done before. I unseated a female jockey.

"You lie like you breathe, Nora. Your legs have been around a lot of things but never the back of a horse. If you fell off anything it was the side of a bar."

Phyllis laughed again, but this time it was more like cold rain.

Nora grabbed her purse and slipped off to the ladies room while Phyllis downed the last of her Gin Ricky.

"Why did you have to go and be so awful?" Phyllis said.

A shade was drawn over Phyllis' eyes and I wondered why I had ever tried to sell her a snappy comment or let myself think about her pretty lips.

I imagined Phyllis on Christmas morning, stuffing her mouth with sweets and forgetting all about the ham-fisted nobody she had met at The Jefferson. I thought about how that same tomorrow would find me sitting at the window above the Five-and-Dime, smoking my Lucky Strikes and listening to Nora say, "It's just another day."

"It's all lies, Phyllis. Can't you see? She's making fools of us."

Phyllis turned toward the bar and I saw in the mirror that her face had fallen.

"It's only you who's the fool, Charlie. Nobody comes to The Jefferson on Christmas Eve because they are interested in the truth about things. Sometimes people just like to be sold a good story."

Phyllis walked off without a backward glance and returned to her three companions at the table.

I was already feeling pretty rotten about everything, but Slim was next in line to the punching bag. He looked at me like I had just kicked a kitten and said,

"You know what, Charlie? You should thank god that you have a Ma like Nora. She frets about you, see? Says you're so sour she's not sure what you'll do when she dies and it's just you and your Lucky Strikes for company. She came in here yesterday and told me to look out for a young lavender she could possibly send your way."

I knew Slim was the worst kind of liar, so I didn't know what to believe. It didn't sit right with me, him talking about Nora dying and calling me a dyke as plain as day.

"You don't know me from Adam, Slim Bobby."

"Don't know that I'd want to, Charlie."

Nora came back to the table and she had fixed her face so you'd never guess the fuss she had made not ten minutes before. She looked at me with a familiar regret and said,

"Nobody likes a stick in the mud, Charlie. Can't you pretend to be some way else for a day in your life? It's Christmas, for god's sake."

My skull pounded and I wished she would make up her goddamn mind about how I was supposed to be.

"Let yourself go a little, Charlie. Let folks see your sparkle."

I thought of myself sparkling; stroking my ring, sipping my Gin Ricky, and dancing home to swing the trapeze with a nice gal that I met at The Jefferson. I thought of old Nora, back in the saddle and finally riding free in to the Pocono sunset. I hung there for a brief second and felt what it might be to live as someone different. The temptation to stay there was something awful, but you wouldn't catch me making myself into a lie.

"Ain't no sparkle, Nora, when a jewel is fake."

Nora turned around, leaned her elbows on the bar, and started to scan the room. I looked at the way the skin collected around her eyes, thought about what Slim had said about her dying, and felt a shiver run through me.

Nora considered the desperate faces assembled in The Jefferson, and I realized that she had not finished her Christmas shopping. She was scanning those paltry offerings for a racehorse; one for her best girl to ride on through to the finish line. It was my turn, then, to feel regret because I suddenly knew I'd never win that race. In the end, the only female jockey in the room was Nora.

"I wish I could ride a horse like you, Nora, but I'm afraid I'll never be able to shake the notion that we are a just pair of dirty old birds who can't fly farther than a couple of rooms above the Five-and-Dime."

Nora reached over, grabbed my swollen fingers, and looked at me like she almost liked me.

"That may be," Nora said, "but it's all pretty unsatisfactory."

"Female Jockeys"

KATE FELIX is an independent filmmaker from Ontario, Canada. She is a purveyor of dark comedy and her small daughter describes her as being "like a rainbow, but with one stripe made of blackness." Her work has been published in the *Bath Flash Fiction Anthology* and the *Cauldron Anthology*, and she recently won the LGBT Toronto screenwriting competition.

She says: "The seed for this story came from a trip I took to New York City with my mom and the tall tales she told to some fancy-looking stranger who sat beside her in a restaurant. It got me thinking about how people's intentions are more interesting than their facts, and how most times you should just cut folks some slack and let them enjoy their own souls. (Also, my mom wants me to mention that she is *nothing* like old Nora, and whatever story I've sold myself about that afternoon is likely the product of my own wild imagination.)"

Genesis

I WAS LEANING against the bar in a speakeasy on 52nd street, waiting for Nora to finish her Christmas shopping, when a girl got up from the table where she had been sitting with three other people and came over to me. She looked young, but I couldn't gauge her age. She had to be at least twenty-one, I told myself, to be in the bar.

But that was an illogical thought.

Maybe I am not that logical. Nora always says I don't think in straight lines. I should check what she means by that. I have always assumed she meant I am eccentric, creative maybe. But that doesn't sound much like Nora, really. She's not romantic in the way she thinks about people. Maybe I just like to think she sees me that way.

I wanted the girl to be over twenty-one, I realized, because she was looking directly into my eyes as she walked over. Not that it mattered. What would I do if I knew for certain she was over twenty-one, anyway? Smile more? Still, it's nice to know where you stand; what tone you are allowed to use, that kind of thing.

"Do you have a Spark?" she asked.

"What?" I looked around me. "No, I don't work here."

"Yeah. That's obvious." She had an accent, I couldn't place it. A little southern but also something else. I can't get the hang of America, with all their states and accents and retrogressive laws with ludicrous loopholes.

Geographically we were located on the second floor of a building in New York City, but *officially* we were standing in the Embassy of the greater Dogstar Nebula. It was one of those pseudo countries that was made up by radical Libertarians back in the Twenty-first Century. Each embassy was still recognized as legally independent, and those that were still around were worth a fortune. The Dogstar Embassy in Berlin was used for old-fashioned stock gambling. Only in America would it be used for something people all over Europe did every day.

The girl was smiling at me. She had freckles which creased into her smile lines.

"I meant, do *you* have a Spark," she said. "You know, like a real one?"

"One of my own?" I liked her smile, it was like wheat fields or something. "God, I don't know if I have any Sparks in me. I'm too old to be inspired by anything."

She laughed. It was a complimentary laugh. Meant to make me feel younger. "You're serious?" I asked when she stopped.

"Yeah. Of course."

"Pure, unfiltered. Just like that?"

"Why not? That's how it's meant to be, right? That's how it used to be before they started messing around with them."

"Right." My mind raced. "Is that even legal? For me to give you a Spark, I mean?"

She laughed again.

"You're asking me *that*, in *here?* Look, I want some inspiration and they don't have any. Actually, they won't serve me anything here today. But who even really wants their stuff? It's so flat and over processed."

She must be under twenty-one then, I thought. That's why they wouldn't serve her.

"But we aren't outside international law. Look, even in Europe you have to do a cursory screening."

"Europe is obsessed with safety. And actually it *is* legal

in the state of New York: interactions between individuals is a private matter. As long as I don't pay you, it's fine. And you're a tourist, right?"

"Is it that obvious?"

"I have an eye for it. That's even better. They can't arrest you for downloading or uploading if it's legal in your country."

Of course I knew that. I was just buying some time to figure out if I wanted to. Or maybe just to keep her talking.

"I'm married. Does that make a difference?"

I don't know why I said that. I always feel I have to mention being married early on. As if I'm scared some beautiful woman is going to fall in love with me if I don't tell them about Nora in the first ten minutes of our conversation.

She shook her head. "No, why should it? But I'm going to share it with my guy friends, so if you were thinking of offering me a dirty Spark…."

"No. No. Of course not." I flushed and felt suddenly old again. "I just meant … being married means I don't have many independent ones."

"Right."

"Okay." I looked around me. "I don't know if this counts…."

"Sure it does." Her gaze became focused, quieter somehow.

"I saw this dead rat in the street."

"A dead rat. When?"

"Yesterday. It had been run over. A crow had started eating it."

"That's pretty intense."

"I didn't feel intense. I felt…."

"Yeah?"

"As if I suddenly saw the order of things. The meaning

of decay. It was beautiful."

"Beautiful?"

"It's hard to explain."

"You don't have to. I'll take it."

"It's not very interesting."

"I'll let you know."

She pulled her Diode from her forearm and leaned toward me.

"Where do you keep yours?" she asked softly. It made the hairs on my neck stand up. I pointed toward my nape.

"You're old-fashioned." She slipped a hand onto my neck.

I felt her fingers, and nodded as a permission protocol flickered in my mind. I tried to focus on the rat: the matted fur and blood. I tried to block out the despair I had been feeling earlier in the day, the hopelessness at the state of my life. A second later she pulled away and slipped her Diode back in place.

She blinked.

"Wow. That's ... that's profound."

"Really?"

"Yeah. You aren't boring at all ... what's your name?"

"Frank."

"Well, you aren't boring, Frank."

She nodded and turned. I felt suddenly cheated. Like she'd promised me something she hadn't delivered. I wondered what it must have been like for her, to have a raw unfiltered experience of another. It had been so long that I hardly remembered. There was Nora, of course, but that didn't count. I knew every inch of her.

"Hey," I called out after her. "Swap me?" The girl stopped and turned, frowning.

"Huh?"

"Swap me."

My internal sensor beeped in my ear canal, telling me my blood pressure was rising. I shook my head, switching it off.

"You just ask for a women's Sparks, do you?" she said.

"A *clean* Spark," I tried to joke, but realized it came out creepy, especially when she was so young. I hadn't wanted to seem pushy, just a bit cocky maybe. Confident. That's what I wanted her to think I was, confident. "Sorry. Forget I asked."

"It's okay. I was just screwing with you." She shrugged. "I like your thoughts, they're growing on me already. I like the way you see the crow. Let me see ... Yeah. I think I've got something for you."

She walked back up to me. This time she took a Diode from behind her ear. I wondered how that worked: more than one Diode. How would it be possible to programme two into one brain? It must be some new tech I didn't know about. I could never keep up with all the stuff kids were into nowadays.

The girl leaned forward and reached behind my neck again. This time it felt different. Like cool liquid. I shook my head a little as my permission pathways flared. I wasn't used to that with Nora. I had switched her onto full permission years ago. I nodded and felt the trickle of a new pathway slip through my mind.

"There you go, Frank." The girl stood back, looking at me as if I were a project she had just successfully completed. Then she started back towards her friends.

The pull of new memory began colouring the edges of my thoughts. I tried not to slip into it too fast, but I couldn't help myself.

"Wait!" I called after her again as I started to process what she'd just given me. "Is this yours? Your own memory, exactly as it was?"

She glanced over her shoulder at me.

"As much as any memory ever is, Frank. Like your crow — I think it was actually a raven. Don't worry, what I gave you is all me. Promise."

She sat back down next to one of her two companions and immediately started to laugh about something he was saying. I watched her.

I blinked.

"So ... What do can I serve you?" The barman finally had decided to appear.

"Something to go," I managed to say. "For me and my wife, for the Holiday. Snow maybe?"

"Nothing for you now? I've got this new bit in from Japan. Very light: watching the cherry blossoms. It's synthetic, of course, but not cheesy."

"No. I'm good."

I tried to focus as the new thoughts slipped around mine as I looked over at the girl. She was leaning against her friend's shoulder now.

Maybe he was her boyfriend.

Then again, maybe he was her son.

The barman followed my gaze and swore.

"Did you just get a free hit of Anne? Sheesh! That woman will take me out of business."

"Anne?" I asked, only half aware of him.

"Her." He gestured to the girl.

She wasn't a girl, I realized. She was a woman. I remembered that now.

"Be careful, she's a junkie. And no ordinary junkie: she has so much of other people's brain in her it's a wonder she can stand upright. You could have got a double from her: a memory of another person's memory, and that from another person. You'll end up feeling like you're in a hall of mirrors, each reflection different. You can even forget who you are for a moment. It makes most people throw up."

I looked over at the mirror behind him. I was definitely still me.

"I think this one's okay. Is she … an actress or something?" I tried to make sense of my memories.

"Anne Quint? You never heard of her?"

I shook my head.

"I won't say anything then."

I ordered a couple of smooth-looking synthetic memories and toyed with the idea of getting one real one. Well, almost real.

You couldn't buy unfiltered memories, even in an illegal joint, it was too dangerous. It hadn't always been. Or, more like, there was just a time we hadn't realized the risks.

When memory extending first hit, we didn't realize just how much information came with a few seconds of thought; how much background noise. We were sharing things we never meant to share, learning things we didn't want to know.

They couldn't undo the technology so they figured out how to clean memories, put filters on them. They watered them down and started making safer, synthetic, ones.

I nodded a thank you to the bartender and took a seat at a small table in the corner of the room.

The truth was I hadn't switched a hit with anyone but Nora for ten years. Not raw. Other than her it had just been educational transcripts for work projects, and entertainment ones, of course. I don't know why. Everyone else I know sneaks hits with other people. Even Nora does. But I hate having another man's memory in me, it always feels wrong, and I can't just ask a woman.

Or wouldn't usually.

Maybe I'm a prude. What is it Nora says about me and girls? I forget.

I blinked.

"…and then I realized we got one from her last year, so I had to go back and exchange it. What happened to you? You look like someone just slapped you."

Nora was settling herself in the chair opposite me, slipping her bag off her shoulder and unpinning her hat from her hair.

"I got a Spark," I admitted.

"What, here? They sell Sparks here?"

"Inspiration? In New York? No. Even if they did we couldn't afford one. I got it off a woman who was here."

"A woman … are you mad? You could have your bank emptied."

"I don't have any money, remember?"

"You know what I mean."

"I'm sure I'll be fine."

Nora looked doubtful.

"Where is she?"

I looked for her but the table she'd been at had a young couple at it now.

"She's gone. Someone called Anne Quint. An actress or something. That's what I get from her memory."

"Don't be stupid, Frank. It wasn't Anne Quint."

"Why? Who is she?"

"She is … was … Anne Quint. The big memory star? She was huge years ago in Beijing. China is flooded with her memories. She made her fortune and got kicked out of the country."

"Why?"

"You seriously don't know?"

I shook my head.

"What did she look like?'

"She was a red head, light red hair, blue eyes, freckles."

"Jesus. That sounds like Anne Quint. Take your time with that memory, it might carry a punch. That's one intense woman."

"Why, was she a dealer or something?"

"No, Frank! How do you live with your head in the

clouds? She was a spy! Back when they used to recruit people for emoting skills. She used to mess with memories and pass them on, like a virus, changing people's feelings about things. That was the theory back then, remember? That we could be brainwashed through other people's memories. Never worked of course, pure quackery."

"Wait. You're talking about the Beijing Hooker?"

"Yes, Anne Quint."

"That was *her?*"

"Maybe. She'd be about sixty, though."

"She must have had her telomeres reversed or something. She looked ... ageless."

"Well, she's rich. She was an early memory boomer. Made a fortune. What the hell did she give you? Pass it over!"

"No." I leaned back, surprised at how protective I felt of it. "It's mine."

"Don't be so childish."

I shook my head. Nora always got what she wanted. She had the job and the money and all the friends. I wanted this for myself.

"Well. Fine then, tell me."

"Uh ... It's an old memory. She's leaving a fancy hotel. Not in Beijing though, somewhere less developed. She bought a pastry for breakfast on the way out. She's late but she decides to walk. She's wearing these pale blue high heels; they squelch in mud. It's been raining and it smells like wet dust. She pulls the pastry out to eat. It's a *pain au chocolat*. She's really hungry. She missed eating the night before because she was up composing something with a man. They flirted but no more. She's regretting it. She's wondering if she'll keep wasting all her opportunities just because she's worried about being seen as a cheap lay. She starts to eat the pastry. It's delicious. And then this woman steps out in front of her; a beggar. She asks for something, but Anne's got no cash and is late and she's hungry, so she tells the woman to go away."

"Charming."

"And then the woman asks for her food. And she gets angry and walks on."

"Right. So she's a rude rich woman?"

"That's what she thinks after a few steps. It was an expensive pastry but she can get something cheaper. So she turns back and retraces her steps, but the woman is gone."

"She looks for her?"

"No. She decides to be late and takes this long way to her destination, through streets overgrown with trees. She keeps thinking about this woman. She thinks about how selfish she was and wonders how the woman feels. She wishes she could let the woman know she saw her, noticed her."

"And?"

"She decides she has to do something to change herself; to be a better person."

"That's it?"

"It's very poignant, it's as if the world just stands still as she walks."

"I don't get it."

I sighed. Nora was always so literal.

"Here." I pulled my Diode off and leaned over to her.

Nora blinked.

"I think I know that city!" she said after a few seconds. "I'll have to look it up."

"But what do you think about the rest?"

"Some spoiled woman with an eating disorder having guilt about being rude to a starving beggar? Who the hell cares?"

I cared.

I felt like Anne had tried to tell me something by giving

me that memory.

"An international spy gives you a straight Spark and this is all you get?"

I frowned at Nora. Why was it that I had never noticed how callous she was before?

I remembered the pinch of those blue shoes, the heavy moisture in the air. I remembered wondering what it means to be kind, where it really starts, why it's so hard.

"We can be kinder though, can't we?" I murmured.

"What's that?"

I smiled, absently, not really knowing why I'd said it.

"The Beijing Hooker went rogue, didn't she?" I asked

"That's right. She got dumped by both sides."

"What did she do?"

"I can't remember the details. Something weird. She tried to plant her own stuff, I think. Had some agenda of her own."

I looked over at the table where the couple were now sitting.

"Would it be that much harder to be kind? We all try, don't we? We think we do, anyway. So why isn't the world kinder?"

"What are you talking about?"

I don't explain myself well. Nora always says ... something. She says something about me. Maybe it doesn't matter what she says.

"I think this memory was important to her somehow," I said. "Like it started something."

"But *nothing* happens," Nora complained. "She doesn't get kissed, or find the woman. She just gets existential. It doesn't go anywhere. It's so frustrating."

"Maybe that's what makes it so important."

"That may be," Nora said, "but it's all pretty unsatisfactory."

"Genesis"

Shanta Gyanchand is a writer and care consultant in Pune, India. "Genesis" is her first published story, and the winner of this year's Hammett contest. We loved the story's imaginative conceit and the interplay of its characters; and Hammett's final line was the perfect "moment of truth" for Frank's relationship with his wife. It was a joy to read and a pleasure to award.

She says: "I found the challenge of this competition's premise intriguing. The specific setting of the Hammett piece appealed to me; the image of a narrator waiting for a woman made me think about what a person, especially a partner, becomes to us when they are absent versus when they are present, and how this makes us feel about ourselves and the world. I attempted to explore this as I wrote, and science fiction always strikes me as being the simplest mode for exploring philosophical ideas. That said, I mostly aimed to tell a compelling story and hope I achieved this."

Nora's Anniversary Present

I WAS LEANING against the bar in a speakeasy on 52nd street, waiting for Nora to finish her Christmas shopping, when a girl got up from the table where she had been sitting with three other people and came over to me.

Every inch of her was painted, and she stood close enough for me to smell the perfume emanating from her skin, close enough that I could count each one of her spidery eyelashes. She was a flower, and I was a honey bee. "You got a light?" she asked.

"I don't smoke."

"Oh?" She raised a penciled eyebrow and placed an unlit cigarette between her crimson lips. "Frightened of a little fire?" she asked.

"Not at all," I said, "but my wife won't allow it."

"Is that so?" she leaned forward so I could see a great deal more of her pale chest than was publicly decent, "And is that something you enjoy? Letting women tell you what to do?"

I ran my finger along the bar. "It can be," I said.

"I'm Rebecca," she said. She clasped her polished nails around my neck and pulled me towards her like a praying mantis going to bite the head off of her lover. Instead, she drew my ear to her lips: "I didn't come over because I needed a light. I want you to meet some friends of mine."

I followed her to the dark corner booth where she introduced her friends, two skinny blonde things who looked like carbon copies of each other were introduced as

Alice and Tina. The third person was a burly gentleman in a suit with a dark mustache and darker eyes. "I'm Robert," he said.

"Tom."

"Sit down, Tom."

I did so. I'm a bank manager, most people wouldn't dare give me an order. Was it anger that made my heart start to beat double-time?

"You've probably guessed why we've brought you over here."

Did I dare say what I was thinking? "I may have."

What might have been a smile stirred beneath Robert's moustache. "Would you like me to explain?"

"Please."

Robert's onyx eyes noted my suit — black, pin striped, tailored to fit. "You look like a man who appreciates the finer things in life." He draped an arm around one of the blondes, Tina possibly. "We're alike in that regard, but everyone in this world has different tastes." He swirled the crystal glass in his hand so the liquid glinted gold in the light of the dim bulb above. "Personally, I have a taste for scotch, among other things." He put down his glass and clutched the neck of a tall green bottle in the centre of the table. "Alice has a taste for champagne," he explained. "Tina, tell Tom what your tastes are."

"I have a taste for…." Tina giggled, and pointed through the table, obviously towards my pants.

"Well, Tom, would you like Tina to suck your…?"

This couldn't be happening. There was *no way* I could, even if I wanted to. I looked around. "My wife —"

"— Has all of Fifth Avenue and your ample wallet at her disposal. She won't return for hours. You can speak freely. I ask again: Would you … like Tina. … to suck … your…?"

"*Yes.*" I felt like a schoolboy admitting to having broken a window.

"And would you like to suck mine while Alice watches?"

"Yes," I said, writhing in my seat, "oh, God, *please*, yes!"

"*Shhh, shhh...,*" Rebecca said, putting her hand in my crotch and stroking as though she were trying to calm a spooked pony. She pulled out a lighter and lit her cigarette with one hand while the other continued to caress me. The lighter was rectangular and metallic, in the dim light it was hard to make out the details, but the shape was familiar. In fact, it was iconic.

"Is that a Zippo lighter?" I asked, through gasps of pleasure.

"Sure is, pumpkin."

I pulled away slightly, "Well, how is that possible?" I said, "This is 1930 and Zippo lighters are not going to be invented until 1933."

Rebecca rolled her eyes. "Can't you just enjoy this?"

I stood up. "No, no. How can I possibly enjoy this when you have entirely taken me out of the scene."

Robert sighed. "Not this again."

"For fuck's sake, Tom," said Alice.

"How is this *my* fault?" I said, "Rebecca is the one who hasn't properly done her research."

"Oh, fuck off, Tom." Rebecca said, "This is a sex club, not the fucking Smithsonian. Why do you care so much?"

"I can't come without a little realism."

"Well, *I* can't come if I'm thinking more about historical accuracy than my own orgasm."

Nora must have heard the commotion and thought we were up to the climax of the scene as she burst through the door at that moment with her arms full of Macy's bags. Her cheeks were red from the cold and she even had snowflakes on the shoulders of her fur coat. It had been snowing on December 15th, 1930, in New York. The woman's attention to detail never failed to arouse me.

When she saw I was not in the throes of passion, Nora

lowered her bags with a disappointed look. "What happened?" she said.

"Rebecca used a Zippo lighter," I explained.

"But Zippo lighters weren't invented until 1933."

"I know."

Nora scratched her pin curls. "I see."

"Can't we just keep going?" Alice asked.

Tina shrugged. "It's a little ruined now, don't you think?"

"Oh come on," Robert said. "It's not like this place was cheap to rent, it feels like someone should at least get sucked off."

"And by someone, do you mean *you*?"

"Well, it wouldn't fucking hurt," Robert muttered.

Rebecca rubbed her temples and sighed. "This isn't going to work," she said.

"I think I'll have to agree," said Nora, "I know you're a fan of the fashion, Robert, but I think Prohibition-era New York was probably overly-ambitious for the group."

"That's *not* what I meant," Rebecca said. "I meant it isn't going to work *with the two of you*."

"What's that supposed to mean?" I said.

"This is a sex club!" Rebecca said, "When is the last time any of us actually had any sex?"

"There was that time with all of the yoghurt," I said.

"That was an exception."

"What if we just take a step back from period scenes?" Nora said.

"We tried that," Tina sighed.

"Tom kept going on about safety procedures during the electrician scene," Robert complained.

"And he completely ruined our *Lord of the Rings* fantasy with that shit about the orcs."

"Well, if you had read the *Silmarillion* —" I began.

"I'm sorry," Rebecca said, "but you're out."

"Since when are you the leader of this group?" I said, "You don't get to just dictate who comes and goes!" Rebecca raised an eyebrow.

I was starting to get really angry until I felt Nora's gentle touch on my arm. "Let's go, Tom," she whispered, and so we did.

But I didn't let it go. I was infuriated, but also a little scared. Nora was a wonderful wife and mother but she was not the type of woman to be satisfied with being only those things. She needed excitement. It was our 10th anniversary coming up, so I decided I was going to do a scene for her, one with all of the realism and ingenuity that our scenes with the club had lacked. I began to spend my every waking moment, outside of work, planning for our next scene. Despite my exhaustion I was getting very in depth with my research, nothing less would do. Nora and I had already converted our basement into a sex dungeon some years ago, so that was helpful and we are quite well off financially so I wasn't finding it too difficult to source and purchase torture devices from my chosen era. My only struggle was finding an actor to fill the final role in the scene. I had looked around the internet and there were many people offering services, but I was hardly willing to risk the success of the evening on some stranger. Rebecca had promptly told me to fuck off when I had rung her, and the others in the group wouldn't even answer my calls.

You can imagine my surprise then, when I came home one afternoon on my lunch break and heard the murmur of Alice's soprano voice mingled with Nora's soft alto. I had only known Alice in the capacity of performing sexual favours, so that is where my mind first went. My instinct was to burst through the door in a jealous red-hot rage, catching them in the act of their embrace. But as I neared I smelt coffee and realised the murmurs were not sighs of passion but the gentle chatter of women in conversation.

"Have you thought about going back to school?" Alice was asking. "If you got your PhD you could easily get a job at a museum or something."

A job? Nora would never need a job. I provided her with all she could possibly want.

Nora sighed. "It's been ten years since I did my masters. I just don't know if I've got it in me anymore. Also I've got little Maxy to consider now."

"All the more reason to go for it. Max needs a role model in his life."

"He has Tom," Nora said.

Alice said nothing in response, but I could picture the look on her face.

"He's a good man," Nora insisted.

"Is he?" Alice asked, "Is he good to you? Because he doesn't seem that way. I'm going to be honest with you, Nora, I've got no idea how you live with the man, the way he obsesses over stupid little details at the club I can only imagine what he's like at home."

"He's trying," Nora said.

"He's a control freak, Nora. He's controlling you."

"No, you don't understand Tom and me. We have a dominant-submissive relationship; it works for us."

"That should stay in the bedroom where it belongs. If not, then it's not a dominant-submissive relationship; it's just an abusive relationship."

"No. There's no abuse, it's just our way of loving each other."

That's right, I thought. It's love.

Alice sighed. "Anyway, the group is having a meeting next week. We're planning a big mermaid and pirates fantasy. We're bringing in some new members to really round it out. I've spoken with the others and you are more than welcome to come along if you'd like."

"But not Tom."

"Not Tom."

"I'll have to think about it."

I left the house sweating. Nora and I were man and wife. We were bonded. I could not lose her. I would not. I would do anything to keep her. I didn't go back to work that day but to another office downtown, my last resort.

"Come in," Robert called. As I stepped into his office, his face immediately turned to stone. "Tom."

I smiled. "Robert, how have you been?"

"Fine."

"The others? Rebecca? Tina?"

"They're all fine." A pause. "Look, if you don't mind I prefer not to discuss my private life at work. Is there a reason you're here?"

"Yes, I was actually hoping you could help me out."

"I can't get you back in the group."

"I know that, that's fine. It's actually Nora."

That piqued his interest. "What about Nora?"

"She's a remarkable woman, Robert."

"She is."

"Our anniversary is this weekend and I want to do a scene for her, a Medieval dungeon fantasy. After all she does for me and Maxy I think it's the least I can do. The problem is I'm short one person."

"And you want me to do it?"

"I have no one else." He seemed unsure. "I just want to give Nora a wonderful anniversary."

"Listen, Tom, I'd be happy to help you out for Nora, but do you really think this is what she wants? Nora strikes me as the type of lady who would be happy with flowers and chocolates."

I shook my head. "You don't know her like I do. I just

want her to feel sexy. It's been hard for her to feel like that after she had our son."

"And you can't make her feel sexy without a Medieval dungeon?"

"When Nora and I met she was writing her thesis on the architecture of Medieval French castles. She'll love it. Trust me."

Robert seemed unconvinced. "I'm not going to ruin it for you with all of my historical inaccuracies?"

"You can't possibly … you'll be gagged."

I eventually got Robert to agree. I think he would have agreed to anything if there was the chance of someone twisting his nipples, but as he stepped inside my townhouse on Friday evening he looked uncertain again. There's something a little satisfying about seeing someone physically stronger look so helpless.

Robert was pretty used to the BDSM scene so it probably wasn't my outfit of leather straps and chains that unsettled him; more likely it was my incongruity with the surroundings. Our house is very neat. Modern and clean without feeling cold and unlived in. It's nice. It's normal.

Robert's dark eyes flitted about like an injured sparrow before coming to rest on a framed photograph on the wall. It showed my son Max sitting next to a cake shaped like a train, his grin was smeared with chocolate. "Is that your son?" Robert asked.

"That's my little boy," I said. "Of course, he's a little bigger than that now, but he still loves his Thomas the Tank Engine. Shall we go to the dungeon?"

"Might as well get started."

I led Robert to the door under our stairs that opened into our dungeon. It was quite beautifully designed. It was fitted out with stone walls which I'd had put in under the guise of making it into a wine cellar. On the wall hung chains and an array of torture devices, numbering in the hundreds. For today's purpose I had removed all items which would not have been available in Medieval France.

"You really are into all this stuff, huh?"

"Mmmm. If you wouldn't mind removing your clothes."

"Oh, yes, of course."

Once Robert was undressed I began to restrain his body to the wall with the straps that hung there. When all of his limbs were in place I reached for the gag. It was actually a wooden bit, designed for using with horses, but it would suit my purpose nicely.

"Now," Robert said, "if I'm going to be gagged, I obviously won't be able to say a safe word, so perhaps we should agree on some sort of 'safe movement,' as it were. A series of blinks, possibly?"

"Oh, the mistress doesn't believe in safe words," I said.

"What do you me—" the rest of Robert's words were muffled by the chunk of wood I had stuffed into his mouth.

"*Shhh*," I whispered, tightening the straps around the back of his head. "Be a good boy, it's easier that way."

Nora was due home at 6 after dropping Maxy off with my parents. She was punctual as always. I heard her keys as she lay them on the hall stand. "Tom?" She called. I didn't say anything, she would know where to find me. As soon as the basement door swung open Robert began to scream into his restraints, though whether he was attempting to warn Nora or get her help I guess we'll never know.

As Nora reached the bottom of the stairs and stepped into view she appeared quite out of place. A middle-aged Mum dropped into a seedy sex den. "Tom?" she said, "Is that Robert? What's going on?"

I knelt on the floor and bowed my head. "Mistress, I have brought you an anniversary gift."

She walked over to Robert and stared at him in his

restraints. "And what am I supposed to do with this?" she asked.

My insides began to twist with nerves and I prayed I wouldn't piss myself this time. "I've prepared a torture scene," I said, mostly managing to keep my voice from trembling. "It's set in Medieval France."

"Medieval France? Like my thesis? Oh, Tom that's so sweet." She walked over to where the instruments hung on the wall and surveyed them. She scowled. "Too bad you've made such a mess of it." I heard Robert's muffled cry of surprise just before I felt the burning lash across my back. I fell to the ground in pain.

"What did I just hit you with, Tom?"

My ears gushed with the sound of my own pulse. Not again. I wondered how much money it would take to buy Robert's silence. Maybe none at all. Nora could be very persuasive.

"I said, W*hat did I just hit you with?*"

"I don't know!" I wailed.

Razor sharp leather slashed into my face, a series of little cuts. "More familiar this time?" she asked. I began to sob. "Would you like another guess?"

Through my tears and the blood running down my face I managed to catch a glimpse of the device Nora held in her hands. "It's a cat o' nine tails!" I cried.

"A cat o' nine tails?" Nora said, "But that can't be, this is Medieval France! When was the cat o' nine tails invented, Tom?"

I sobbed, "During the Napoleonic Wars." *How could I have been so stupid?*

"So why is it here?"

"I don't know, mistress. I'm sorry."

"What are you sorry for? Sorry you don't love me enough to do your research properly?"

"I tried my best, I really did."

Nora ran her finger along another device on the wall, a long one with metal spikes. "That may be," Nora said, "but it's all pretty unsatisfactory."

"Nora's Anniversary Present"

MOLLY WILSON is an assistant store manager at a pet shop. She's Australian, but lives in New Zealand, and like most twenty-four-year-olds, she's happy to tell you she has no idea what the hell to do with her life. "Nora's Anniversary Present" is her first published story.

She says: "I wasn't going to write this story. The beginning sentence — it just seemed way too restrictive. It had to be set during prohibition and, most likely, it had to be set in New York. I am far too much of a pedant to write a story full of historical inaccuracies; but I am also far too lazy to do my research. Plus, I didn't want to write a story set in the 1930s. And this story obviously had to be set in the 1930s. But then I thought, well, maybe it didn't...."

Me and Mimi

I WAS LEANING against the bar in a speakeasy on 52nd street, waiting for Nora to finish her Christmas shopping, when a girl got up from the table where she had been sitting with three other people and came over to me. I recognised her instantly. Of course I did. She was me. Twenty years younger, but me all the same. I groaned. It had happened again. Nora was going to hit the roof.

The girl, young me, said, "You've got to concentrate."

"I *was* concentrating," I said. "Your wife was taking too long with the shopping."

"No, she wasn't. You're — we're — just impatient. I thought I'd grow out of that by the time I hit —" she looked me up and down "— fifty?"

"Rude," I said. "I'm forty-two."

She winced. "I should enjoy these good years then, huh?" I was gorgeous then. Smoking Marlboro reds and insisting that everyone call me Mimi. This girl, Mimi, was a stranger to me and the look she gave me of withering pity was something I would never clean from my retinas.

"Am I the oldest?" I said.

"No, an eighty-year-old us slipped through a few months ago. Funny old broad. Sharp as a needle."

We looked at each other. Two people sharing a future as a sharp old lady.

"Am I the youngest?" She said.

"No, I was watching a documentary about salt two weeks ago and the next minute I was in our old house on

Cooper's Lane and saw baby us."

She smiled, showing all of her perfect white teeth. "Wow. Baby us. Were we gorgeous?"

"We were. Chubby little cheeks and legs like big sausages."

"Cool."

The urge when these little slips happen is to give my young self warnings and lotto numbers. I never did. The lotto numbers wouldn't work, and the warnings would be considered for a day and forgotten after a bath and good night's sleep. How do you tell a teenager to be careful about who she falls in love with? She's not going to listen/care/not date the girl with the motorcycle, so the whole thing is moot.

"I wanted to give you some advice," she said with a look of grave solemnity on her unblemished, unwrinkled face.

I laughed, "Really?"

"Advice from eighty-year-old us."

"Oh yeah, what did she have to say?"

"She slipped through while Nora was Christmas shopping."

My heart flipped in my chest. When I'm eighty I'll still be shopping with Nora. Tears filled my eyes and I ignored them.

"She slipped through and I was on a date with a girl called Suzy."

I smiled, "First or second date?"

She blushed. "Second."

We smiled at each other. A conspiratorial smile as we remembered our night with Suzy. "Anyway, old-as-hell us walks into the bar and, same as you, I spotted she was me straight away. I went over, and she said, 'Honey, all you're gonna need to know is this: love with every fiber of your being, eat at fancy restaurants, travel whenever you can and, most importantly, drink more gin.' Then she gave me a big grandma kiss on the cheek and vanished."

"That's good advice."

"I wanted to pass that on. I know that you should already know it. You should remember it from when you were me, or maybe that's not how time works, but I thought you should know."

"Time travel is the worst."

"Right?! I was in a lecture last week and drifted off. The next minute I was looking at pre-school us that time when we wet ourselves after fighting Johnny Johnson. That was the worst."

I laughed, "Johnny Johnson? I bumped into him a few weeks ago. He's married. Five kids."

She shrugged, "I'm still mad about him making us wet our pants."

"Oh, don't get me wrong. He looked like crap."

"That's a relief."

An awkward silence fell between us. It's weird how people talk all the time about the things they would say if they could speak to themselves when they were younger, but when the time comes you just want to stare at yourself. Here was me in my prime. Young, skinny, confident. This me hadn't had the cancer scare at twenty-five. Hasn't lost her sister in a car accident. Hadn't fallen out with her parents when she finally came out to them. This beautiful creature in front of me literally had my whole life ahead of her and the idea that I would warn her of what came next made me feel ill.

So, we smiled at each other and I said, "You should go back to your friends. They're gonna start asking questions about this broken down middle-aged woman you've been chatting to."

She gave me a wink, "You're looking good, Mimi."

I pulled her in for a hug, "You too, kid."

"Do I call Suzy again?"

"Yeah, but she's ghosting you, so don't get your hopes up."

"Oh, that sucks."

"Her loss." I let go of her.

"Until next time."

I blinked, and she was gone, and I was leaning on the bar again in an empty speakeasy. I ordered another drink.

Nora walked in weighed down by shopping bags.

"Miriam, order me something, honey."

I ordered her a gin and tonic and we sat at one of the many unoccupied tables.

"You keep out of trouble?" she asked after taking off her gloves.

"I slipped again. Met a younger me."

She shook her head. "Remember what doctor Pilgrim said, you need to *concentrate*."

"I know, I know, I know," I stared into my drink. "It's just...." I lost the thought as I began to say it and neither me nor Nora went in search of it.

"Was I there?"

"This was pre-you."

She raised an eyebrow. "And here was me thinking you didn't exist until I came into your life."

I smiled at her, "Oh, there is a dark period for those first twenty odd years while I waited for a beautiful woman to emerge out of the fog and demand a gin and tonic."

"Still got the moves, old girl," she said, and I laughed. "Miriam —"

I held up my hand, "Can you call me Mimi? Like you did when we first met."

She chuckled, "Only because you insisted upon it."

"Yeah, I know. But Miriam is a little too —" I twirled my hand in the air as though reeling the right word in.

"Old," said Nora.

"Yeah, something like that."

She shrugged. "Time's arrow only flies in one direction, petal. At least you're not sitting here by yourself drinking gin and tonics with your memories."

"That's very poetic."

"It is. Now if you'll excuse me, I need to pee." She stood up and walked to the back of the bar. I stared into my drink again and felt the corners of my vision crease up as though I was falling asleep.

I snapped them open and I was no longer in the bar. I was in a hospital room.

There was a woman in the bed, attached to too many machines that beeped and whirred as the woman's chest rose and fell with rattling breaths.

"Nora," I said.

The woman, her face mostly hidden behind an oxygen mask opened her eyes and stared at me. Her shaking hand rose, and she pulled the mask away.

"You … need … to … *concentrate*."

Her face was an atlas of wrinkled mountain ridges and deep valleys. Her eyes were clouded but still sharp and she was, somewhere under all those years, the woman I married.

"I know, love. But, I've got a terrible attention span."

She nodded. "You … did."

"Oh."

My mind and body didn't know how to react to this. There is no experience that prepares you for being told that you've slipped through time into a future where you're dead. You can imagine what it's like to be told a loved one is dead. You can prepare or practice like I did about my parents for years. And then the person dies, and you surprise yourself with improvisations that stray miles away from the script you had been preparing.

"How?" I said. "Or maybe I don't want to know."

"Sky … diving."

"What? Oh my God. Really? No. Are you making fun of me?"

She nodded and let out a wheezing laugh.

"You're ... at ... home."

"Wow. That is actually pretty impressive."

"Still ... got ... it."

"I love you, Nora."

She winked at me.

Fingers snapped in front of my face and I was back in the speakeasy on 52nd street with middle-aged Nora shaking her head at me. "Miriam!"

"I know, I know, I know."

"Next time you do this, take lotto numbers or bring some back."

"I can't, it doesn't work. I can only see people I care about and, I don't know, learn from them or something. It's good, I guess to see how the world moves on and how you're cast along on the stream. It's a way for me to reset and realize that I need to cherish my youth, love my wife, and never go sky diving, just in case."

"So, no lotto numbers?"

"No. Just life lessons and reminders that I love my wife. So hopefully you're happy to continue not being a millionaire."

She rolled her eyes. "That may be," Nora said, "but it's all pretty unsatisfactory."

"Me and Mimi"

SEAN FALLON is an education consultant in Victoria, Australia. He is currently working on a novel about John Wayne running for president, and has had his fiction published in *The Big Issue* and *Reader's Digest*. His submission to the Carroll contest, "The Kitten God Heresy," received honorable mention, as did his submission to the Parker contest, "Sext."

He says: "I was waiting for a meal in a restaurant while on a business trip and I saw this competition on Facebook. As soon as I read the first line of *The Thin Man*, the story jumped into my head pretty much fully formed, and I wrote the first draft on my phone in-between forkfuls of the fish and chips I had for dinner. The biggest struggle for me was the ending. Trying to fit Hammett's words into the story was very tricky and took quite a few tries before I could make it work."

Mateusz Buga

The Ślub Man

I WAS LEANING against the bar in a speakeasy on 52nd street, waiting for Nora to finish her Christmas shopping, when a girl got up from the table where she had been sitting with three other people and came over to me.

"What's with the hat?" she asked. I was wearing a fuzzy black Orthodox hat for my religious conversion before I could marry Nora. I wasn't breaking any rules stopping by the bar. I checked. There was a terrible wind outside and this counted as shelter.

"I'm converting," I replied. I saw our reflection in the shiny metal column that separated the bar. I always looked different than I expected. I expected to see high-minded. Thoughtful eyes. Smart nose. Instead I see a shloob.

Ślub, actually. Pronounced "Shloob." The Polish word for wedding. The first time I heard Nora's parents say it, I thought they were calling me a name. I thought it meant "a dope."

Wesele. Pronounced "veh-seh-leh." Also a Polish word for wedding, and much prettier. But they still used ślub around me. I'm not convinced it wasn't an inside joke. Shloob still meant "a dope" to me, not wedding.

"Converting to what?" she asked.

"Orthodox," I replied. I could see the three friends she left still sitting at their table, and they gave no side glances in our direction or at my hat. Her friend had a hooded jacket on so tight you couldn't see her eyebrows or the divot beneath her bottom lip. It was so cold out so I didn't judge.

I hadn't done much judging at all since I started the conversion rites. I was becoming a better person. It didn't take some internal beckoning or wake-up call. I just needed a set of rules to follow so I could please Nora's parents.

"Is the hat real?" she asked.

"Yes," I replied.

It succeeded as a hat. The fur was fake. Not sure where it was made. I didn't know what aspect's authenticity she was questioning but I didn't want to extend the conversation. If I did anything nice or bad, I'd have to mark it down in my conversion journal, which I could feel sinking in my pocket. I didn't want this meeting in my journal. Then she touched the hat.

Smrod. Pronounced "smroot." That's a Polish word that does a better job than it's English counterpart, "stench." I really identified with that term in the sweaty summer nights, right when I took off the hat before I showered.

"It's so soft!" she said.

I started to sweat like in those hot summer days after five seconds of her rubbing the hat. I wasn't concerned about my emotions or thoughts, I just had to be outwardly proper. I had learned to be more religious than spiritual per Nora's lead. She was begrudgingly polite at all times. I didn't know about a holy spirit.

I drank the rest of the beer in one gulp, which was hard to do since all the beers were strong, per the fashion at the time. I shook it off and left. She shouted something to me but I kept walking until I got outside and the hostile ambient wind drowned out her voice.

I lifted my hat to let some cool air draft in.

"You forgot this!" she yelled. She had followed me out. She held my conversion journal. She flipped through it. I let more of the outside air in under my hat's brim.

"Please don't look through that," I replied.

"Calm down!" she said, "I'm giving it back to you. You

should be thankful."

Spokój się. Pronounced "shpokoy sheh." That's how you say "calm down" in Polish. Nora's family has told me that Polish sounds like the wind because it's consonant-heavy and spoken fast. They meant it romantically, but it's a frigid wind. It might even be strong enough to lift flotsam out of the sea.

"I am very thankful," I said, "God bless you."

"That's the kindest thing you've said yet," she said, "What kind of Orthodox are ya? You're not very nice for one."

"How many Orthodox folks have you met? And I'm Polish Orthodox."

"I thought Polish people were Catholic."

"Not all of them."

She flipped through the journal one more time before handing it over.

"So you're just writing down all the nice stuff you do in here?" she asked.

"And the bad stuff too, so I can repent for it later."

"Who is this?" Nora said. I didn't see or hear her arrive, but she was then standing beside me with two giant shopping bags. She was like a silent pointy cloud. She had a white hat, white shoes, and the bags were white too.

"Just a stranger, I dropped my journal and she returned it."

"Who's that? Your sister?" the woman inserted herself.

"My fiancé," I replied.

"Oh, is that why you're converting? So you're not even a real Orthodox type of person. That explains it," she said.

"Explains what?" asked Nora.

"Nothing. I don't even know her name," I said. It was a strong wind, and it began pushing us away from the woman on the sidewalk's icy veneer.

"We have to go. Thank you for finding my journal," I added before she could tell us her name.

"My name's Helen!" she yelled as we slipped away with the wind. Nora's shopping bags acted as a sail, so I walked faster to keep up with her effortless glide down the sidewalk.

Nora grabbed my journal and thumbed through it. She mouthed "Helen" as she skimmed the pages. She wasn't noticing all the good stuff I wrote down! I let some guy borrow $100 bucks. I always chipped in extra to group restaurant bills and never asked for any back. I didn't ignore the old guy across the street anymore. I knew all about his grandchildren and how he made sure his pipes didn't freeze and burst. I made it through a whole Polish textbook!

The wind kept blowing away everything except for the notebook. Street signs flew through windows. Car tires burnt rubber trying to drive against the wind, but they stayed in place. I held my hat in place with both hands.

"This journal is for you! It's a monument to the man you've made me!" I yelled. The wind had mercy and didn't blow my words away.

"That may be," Nora said, "but it's all pretty unsatisfactory."

"The Ślub Man"

MATEUSZ BUGA is a library administrative assistant from California, in the United States. He used to spin punk and metal records on college radio at 3 am, but now he's a new father who rocks his daughter back to sleep at 3 am. "The Slub Man" is his first published story.

He says: "As a new father and first-generation Polish American, I've been trying to speak Polish to my daughter. My Polish is rusty, so I've come to learn that I've had the wrong understanding of a number of Polish words! It's common among first-generation kids to speak back in English when parents speak their mother tongue, so I never had my word-use corrected. This story is a result of ruminating on accidentally re-defining words based on your personal experiences with them."

Between Two Foothills

I WAS LEANING against the bar in a speakeasy on 52nd street, waiting for Nora to finish her Christmas shopping, when a girl got up from the table where she had been sitting with three other people and came over to me. I turned to see her across the room as if by magnetic attraction. The emerald green gown she was wearing suggested a delicate, yet firm figure. It brushed lightly against her skin, producing a contrast that made her conspicuous amongst men far too consumed by stupor to notice her. She pulled the stool from under the pinewood countertop and brought her left hand toward me, gesturing for help to climb onto it.

Speakeasies were more obscure and murky in Bogotá than they were in the America of Prohibition. They stood mostly to the north of the city centre and lined the busy sidewalks of Thirteenth and Caracas Avenues. The clandestine arms of political parties gathered in the illegal bars of Chapinero, brusquely scribbling onto beer-stained rags of paper the names of opponents to eliminate or intimidate. They bellowed at each other, uttering a barrage of epithets, of which only a handful I found intelligible. Construction workers flooded in after six, wearing a thick paste of sweat and concrete dust on their hands and faces. Scarlet women hired from nearby brothels tended to the sore men, who could barely acknowledge them between tiredness and drunkenness. The room was made a foot lower by the dense fog of smoke from lighted cigars.

I tried to make sense of this beautiful girl's presence in such an unpleasant setting. "It's the one place where my fiancé won't look for me," she intervened, spotting my bemusement. "And also the only business that will sell a woman a proper drink without so much as an interjection."

I paused for a moment, still gazing at her. She took notice and looked down, holding her hands together and resting them on her lap. A flock of her light auburn hair escaped from behind her ears and fell in front of her face, concealing her demure grin. She wore small pearl earrings that could scarcely be made from the faint, almost porcelain-like tone of her skin. My mind wandered for a second before I could speak again.

"I suppose it's only fair that your next one is on me, miss…."

"Eugenia," she replied without hesitation. "Eugenia Descoteaux." She looked back up and placed the hair covering her face back behind her right ear. I smiled and gestured the barman to produce a glass of gin. Eugenia clutched it unassumingly, resting her elbow on the countertop as she brought it to her mouth. The burn of the gin in her throat forced her back into a restrained coquettish demeanour. "I must say, your being here is almost as bewildering as mine," she simpered. I smiled and took a drink of whiskey. "I have things to run away from, as well." She raised her eyebrows. "My sister's shopping and this city's dreadful weather," I added. Eugenia scoffed at my predicament, but maintained her coy attitude, and grinned with only one end of her lips. "A vulgar refuge for such a glamorous problem," she argued. "Why run away from Bogotá's weather? That would mean escaping the comforting cold of the rain, the fog atop the Eastern Hills that consumes their summits and makes them infinite at the same time. It deprives you of the earthy smell after it has rained, the humidity of decomposing tree bark. No, you don't run away from places. You run away from people." Eugenia's tirade rang of lament. It echoed a pain that surrounded her like a miasma. One that she couldn't be sure anyone was aware of but herself.

We sat in an empathetic silence that froze time in the room. The smoke of the cigars trapped the sound waves and asphyxiated them in a dense brume of nicotine and tobacco. The mouths of the patrons swung up and down, but produced no sound, as Eugenia and I looked at each other in accidental complicity. I had lost track of time when the people she had been sitting with walked towards us and let her know they were leaving. Eugenia told them she would catch up with them and descended from the stool. "I will be here at lunchtime tomorrow," she whispered. "I hope you are too. This place isn't nearly as tasteless in the daytime." She took my hand and held it for a moment. As she let go, she slipped a piece of torn cardboard into my breast pocket. Just as gracefully as she had come towards me a few minutes before, she walked away. I followed suit moments later.

The moon rose above the mountains and cast its cold light on the vast stretch of tarmac that lay ahead. I snuggled inside my overcoat and put my hands into the side pockets. The wind seeped in through the seams of the suit. From the top of the mountains to the foothill descended a light fog that scattered the light from the lampposts. Minute specks of glimmering water floated westward. I followed the fog down 52nd Street for a few blocks, turning north once again on Thirteenth Avenue towards the store Nora told me she'd be in.

"Wasn't I supposed to meet you at the bar?" she inquired when she saw me come in. Being my older sister, Nora was quick to notice the thousand-yard stare on my face. "It was far too loud in there," I drawled. Whether out of understanding or disinterest, Nora neglected to ask why I looked nonplussed. She placed her hand on the back of my head and tilted it towards her, kissing me on the forehead. "Help me get the bags. It's late."

Nora and I lived in the corner of 69th Street and 10th Avenue. The façade of the house was blanketed with Japanese ivy. The house itself was built in a style reminiscent of Victorian architecture, as were most houses here. Nora and I entered in silence. I placed the bags by the navy armchair by the front door and walked upstairs. Sitting on my bed, I reached into my breast pocket. Out of it and in my hands was the wrinkled piece of cardboard Eugenia had slipped in. On the back, printed in brown ink was "Scoteaux Fotógrafos." Written hastily on the front were the words "tomorrow we are leaving for the mountains" and "7837, 90th Street, number 7-71."

The note only accentuated my confusion. Not only was the phrase cryptic and lacking in context, the address made little sense. Whether anything further than 85th Street was actually part of Bogotá was debatable. Streets were no longer numbered according to convention and were paved unevenly, if at all. The lands there had been traditionally distant from the city and were home to the country houses of affluent socialites and politicians. Slowly but surely Bogotá grew towards the north, blurring the borders between itself and surrounding villages. Soon, the Bogotá savanna would be one of concrete and asphalt, instead of grasslands and woods.

Having been abducted from the world by Eugenia and her note, I took a blanket from the table next to the wardrobe and lay on the bed, still wearing the thousand-yard stare I put on after she left the bar.

When I woke up the next day, the fog had subsided. The sky went from royal blue in the west to a subtle pink in the east, as the sun slowly rose from behind the Andes. Scattered across were a handful of white traces too small to be clouds. It was Friday and the city brimming with activity. The morning newspaper featured advertising for bullfighting at the Santamaría Bullring, an evening play at the Colón Theatre and a couple of football matches between Bogotá's two main teams and two others from Perú and Costa Rica. I went downstairs and called for Nora but there was no reply. The clock by the front door read half past eight.

The morning went by slowly as I had breakfast and took a shower. I opened the window opposite my bed to let the wind in before leaving. The white lace curtains danced around as the air blew in, projecting their shadow onto the carpeted floor. I sat on the bed for a while, feeling midway between tired and unsettled. The sun was aiming squarely at the open window, having risen above the mountaintops for a couple of hours. It was a quarter to twelve, and time to return to the bar. Reluctant to walk, I took the keys to Nora's Ford Coupé and drove east on 70th Street towards Seventh Avenue.

I arrived at the bar at five past twelve. Indeed, the place looked completely different. Gone were the thugs and bricklayers and the suffocating smoke. Only a few tables were taken by well-to-do businessmen sporting well-tailored suits. The wooden floor was spotless and the light of day displayed the full depth of the establishment. I glanced around and saw Eugenia sitting on the far end of the bar. She wore an off-white blouse and a long navy skirt. Her hair was tied up into a bun. Her face bore a uneasy, impatient expression. No sooner I placed my hand on her shoulder to let her know I'd arrived, she turned and threw herself at me in a relieved embrace. "You really came," she sighed. "You're really here." I held her for a moment, trying to silently reassure her. There was nothing doing

"We need to leave," she urged. "My car is parked just on 53rd Street," I replied. "Let me bring it around." Eugenia refused hastily. "Wait for me there. I'll drive by and you can follow me." She ran out before I could ask any questions. I went outside into the early afternoon sun and glanced at my wristwatch. Ten to one.

It took Eugenia ten minutes to drive by me in an off-white Mercedes 170V. She parked ahead and came to my window. "We are leaving for the mountains," she proclaimed with a hint of resignation. "What's in the mountains?" She looked towards Seventh Avenue with sadness.

"You don't run away from places," she sputtered. "You run away from people. All the people that are here are not in the mountains." The wind blew on her troubled face. A few strands of hair floated in it as she slowly turned back to look at me and back away towards her car.

We drove west on 53rd Street and turned north on Fourteenth Avenue, which led onto the main motorway out of Bogotá. There was little indication of what Eugenia intended to do or where she was going. Tall oaks and weeping willows guarded the motorway as it curved away from the Andes and deep into the savanna. Bogota dissolved into green with each passing mile and Eugenia kept driving north. I followed her for about an hour and a half, going past the town of Guasca and towards Suesca. Her driving matched the calm of the Andes as they opened up either side of the road and formed a valley, but it was far from the urgency and confusion that her words bore before we departed.

Just outside Suesca, Eugenia's driving became erratic. She made a hard right on the edge of the village and went off road onto a strip of natural sandstone cliffs that rose from the earth as if it had been broken in half by the hands of God. I struggled to keep up as she gained speed and the dust from the dirt made it hard to predict her path. Eugenia sped her car inches away from the edge of the cliffs and steered frantically from side to side like she had lost control of it. I could hardly make the Mercedes from behind the cloud of brown dust in front of me, and fought off the pressure building up in my chest as I grew increasingly distressed.

The dust suddenly settled. The Mercedes was nowhere to be seen. I stopped the car and got off to see some faint particles of dirt lead down from the edge of the cliff. I felt an almost electric shock as I ran to see Eugenia's car splattered onto the train tracks that ran along the side of the hills. The roof had collapsed into the body. A light trail of smoke emanated from the crushed bonnet. The shattered glass scintillated as the passing clouds obscured and revealed the sun, casting the shadow of the rocks onto the car. The faces of ancient indigenous monarchs could almost be made from the features of the rocks, guarding the wreck like it was one of them. I rushed back to the car and drove down the cliffs onto the main road. By the time I turned towards the train tracks, a crowd of farmers had gathered. An ambulance from the Suesca Municipal Hospital sped by and into the tracks. The farmers shouted at it with urgency. "She's dead!"

A piercing pain stabbed my chest and twisted it. I turned the car sharply back south.

I drove recklessly towards the city, slaloming in and out of the stalled cars in front of me. The oncoming lane was jammed with traffic. Something had happened in Bogotá. I took Eugenia's torn cardboard out of my pocket. 90th Street, number 7-71. Eugenia had lured me to her suicide outside of the city knowing that something would be awfully wrong when I returned. She had planned for it. She expected me to drive to 90th Street. The weight in my heart was gone. I turned out of the motorway and into one of the unpaved roads that led to Seventh Avenue towards 90th Street. There were plumes of black smoke coming from the south. Bogotá was on fire.

Number 7-71 was an estate like so many in the outskirts of the city. Nobody was around and the gates had been locked with chains. Adjacent to them was a lamppost with a special miniature gamewell. It had a wooden enclosure and a metal lid, embossed with concentric lines and eagle's wings. There was a combination lock above the design. I entered the number 7837. Inside was an unmarked envelope. I put it into my jacket just as a lorry drove by. On the back of it were men carrying Colombian flags and rifles. They were shouting, red with fury. "They have murdered the Republic! Death to the Conservative rats!" Two more went by, each with a payload of irate mercenaries driving towards the city centre where the fires raged and the smoke blackened the sky. Night had fallen upon Bogotá. I had to make sure Nora was safe.

I found Nora barricaded inside our house with Mr. and Mrs. Roberto Schlesinger, our next door neighbours. "They killed Gaitán," she sobbed. "The Liberals are wreaking havoc." I held her in awe. "They did what?" I rushed upstairs into my room and examined the envelope. Hesitating for a moment, I opened it. A flush gold ring fell onto my lap. There was a resting place for what should have been a small diamond. On the inside of the band, an inscription read 'JRS-ED.' It was Eugenia's engagement ring. I set it aside and found a handwritten letter, impeccably folded and sealed with a blue ribbon.

> *Juan,*
>
> *I remember when I first read you Wilson's poems. You were delighted to hear such authenticity in a world where word has been weighed down by ornaments that distort its meaning and conceal it. You said poets and politicians use the same tools of deception. I could not have imagined how close those words were to home.*
>
> *Do you remember the first line I read you, Juan? 'Once I could hold you and the world reflected back at me'? I held you through your bouts of fury and the fairy tales that you made up to keep yourself prone and innocent of your own demise.*
>
> *I can hold you no longer. The world no longer reflects back at me from the glimmer in your eyes. I see in them despair and misled anger. And now you have proven you have the will to translate anger into violence. I cannot wake up in this world that you created. The fire will die out, the dead will be buried, but the bullet wounds of that one man will be the bullet wounds of this country. You brought the night and I shall sleep.*
>
> *May God have mercy on you, because the people of Colombia will not.*
>
> *Eugenia. 9 April 1948*

The pieces started to go together. "Nora, who did this? Who killed Gaitán?" I shouted. Nora sobbed for a minute and then stammered. "The Conservative Police. They are saying on the radio that an officer named Juan Roa Sierra shot him four times, but they don't even know who he is. The Liberals lynched him and dragged his body through Seventh Avenue to the Presidential Palace."

As soon as Nora said the man's name, I felt the cold crash down my spine. "He brought the night," I gasped. Eugenia knew. She knew Colombia would end that day, burdened by the weight of its own existence. I wasn't shaken by the riots, the dead bodies on the streets, the sense that the Republic had died. I was shaken by the actions of the only person that knew and was brave enough to do the only logical thing after being given the fatal gift of clairvoyance.

"At last the lie of Colombia is dead. We didn't deserve to have this place if we couldn't run it," I complained.

Nora looked back in disbelief.

"That may be," Nora said. "But it's all pretty unsatisfactory."

"Between Two Foothills"

JUAN PABLO GONZÁLEZ ARBOLEDA is a writer, musician, and graphic designer, living in Bogotá, Colombia. "Between Two Foothills" is his first published story.

He says: "The Hammett prompt was unmistakably set in New York, which immediately drove me to turn it around and bring the story to my hometown, Bogotá, which uses a similar system for addresses as Manhattan. I wanted to portray the long-lost essence of the city, which died during the *Bogotazo*, murdered by its own people. Seeking to let loose my inexplicable nostalgia for something I never knew, I injected it into the one person who knew it would die. Two impossibilities made into one."

Honorable Mentions

We received nearly one thousand submissions to this year's Literary Taxidermy Short Story Competition, and many impressed both early readers and final judges. In the end some good stories were turned away. The following stories all made it to the last round of selection. Keep an eye out for these writers. We're confident you'll see their work in the future.

Emma Atkins, "Speak Easy, Say Nothing"
Stephen Austen, "Sanctuary"
Tabitha Bast, "Between Whores and God"
Heather Bourbeau, "Red Stone Haunting"
Kim Dicso, "Bookcases and Bullets"
Findlay Donnan, "Plastic Love"
Andrew Dovey, "The Tornado"
Paul D. Erland, "The Slender Thread"
Julie Fitzpatrick, "Old School Ninja"
Nicole Harris, "Poison in the Green Bottle"
Matthew Hauser, "Still Me"
Morgan Jeffery, "A Stranger in the Speakeasy"
Linda Baten Johnson, "An Honest Mistake"
Larry C. Kerr, "Christmas Angel"
Monet Lessner, "What She Wanted to Know"
Samuel Thomas Mannell, "Marmalade"
Carolyn Marguet, "Call Me Gwen"

Jim Mentink, "Triple Scrutiny"
Laura Morley, "The Profusion"
Sarah Pottinger, "Mrs. Giles"
Debbie Robson, "On Fifth Avenue"
Bethany Russell, "10 Cents"
Joanna Carla Santoso, "The Grim Reaper That Abandoned Her Duty"
Michael Seaton, "Better Watch Out"
Michele Thasim, "Buddy and the Girl"
Rhonda Trunnell, "Dames and Demons"
Marie Wilson, "Marty Saves Christmas"

This Year's Judges

Given the eclectic nature of the three opening/closing lines in the 2018 Literary Taxidermy Short Story Competition, and our desire for submissions to span genres, we assembled a group of professional writers and editors from all walks of the literary life. The judges for this year's competition included a poet, a playwright, a mystery writer, a speculative fiction writer, a fantasy writer, a young adult writer, a horror writer, and a food writer. They had a challenging task, separating not only wheat from chaff, but wheat from wheat, and we are grateful for their enthusiastic and perspicacious participation.

Catherine Barnett is the author of three collections of poems: *Human Hours* (2018), *The Game of Boxes* (2012), and *Into Perfect Spheres Such Holes Are Pierced* (2004). Her honors include a Whiting Award, a Guggenheim Fellowship, and the James Laughlin Award from the Academy of American Poets. She has published widely in journals and magazines, including *The New Yorker*, *The Kenyon Review*, and *The Washington Post*. Barnett teaches in the graduate and undergraduate programs at New York University, is a distinguished lecturer at Hunter College. She has degrees from Princeton University, where she has taught in the Lewis Center for the Arts, and from the MFA Program for Writers at Warren Wilson College.

Kelley Eskridge is a fiction writer, essayist, and screenwriter. She is the author of the New York Times

Notable novel *Solitaire*, a finalist for the Nebula, Endeavour, and Spectrum awards. The short stories in her collection *Dangerous Space* include an Astraea prize winner and finalists for the Nebula and Tiptree awards. Eskridge's story "Alien Jane" was adapted for an episode of the SciFi channel series Welcome to Paradox. Her film *OtherLife* (2017) is currently streaming on Netflix. She is a former vice president of Wizards of the Coast, the company responsible for the collectible trading games *Magic*™ and *Pokémon*™. She earns her keep as a corporate learning professional, as well as an independent editor with an international client list of established and emerging writers. She lives in Seattle with her wife, novelist Nicola Griffith.

Stephen Graham Jones is a Blackfeet author of experimental fiction, horror fiction, crime fiction, and science fiction. He has published in everything from literary journals to truck-enthusiast magazines, from textbooks to anthologies to best-of-the-year annuals. Jones has been an NEA Fellow, a Texas Writers League Fellow, and has won the Texas Institute of Letters Award for Fiction and the Independent Publishers Multicultural Award. His areas of interest, aside from fiction writing, are horror, science fiction, fantasy, film, comic books, pop culture, paleoanthropology, technology, and American Indian Studies. Jones received his BA in English and Philosophy from Texas Tech University (1994), his MA in English from the University of North Texas (1996), and his PhD from Florida State University (1998).

Holly Kowitt has written more than fifty books for younger readers, including *The Fenderbenders Get Lost in America*, *This Book Is a Joke*, *This Dance is Doomed*, and *The Principal's Underwear is Missing* (a brilliant update of PG Wodehouse's *Jeeves and Wooster*, set in a suburban high school). She also wrote and illustrated the bestselling LOSER LIST series, which has been translated into ten languages. She grew up in Evanston, Illinois and graduated from Brown University. A former editor at Scholastic Books, she lives in New York City, where she enjoys cycling, flea markets, and West Coast swing dancing. She spends most days writing and drawing in her art studio in Harlem.

Brian Parks is an American playwright, journalist, and editor. He lives in New York City and served as the Arts & Culture editor at *The Village Voice*, as well as Chairman of the Obie Awards. As a playwright, Brian has produced works that are noted for their dark comedy and fast pace. Best known for his play "Americana Absurdum" (which consists of the two shorter plays, "Vomit & Roses" and "Wolverine Dream"), his other works include "Goner," "Suspicious Package," "Out of the Way," "The Invitation," and "Imperial Fizz." "Americana Absurdum" was honored with the Best Writing award at the 1997 New York International Fringe Festival and a Scotsman Fringe First Award at the 2000 Edinburgh Festival Fringe. He is currently Senior Editor at *4Columns*, a website of arts criticism aimed at a general audience.

Michael Pronko is a mystery writer, essayist, and teacher, born in Kansas City, but living and writing in Tokyo for the past twenty years. He has published three award-winning collections of essays: *Beauty and Chaos: Essays on Tokyo*; *Motions and Moments: More Essays on Tokyo*; and *Tokyo's Mystery Deepens*. His award-winning mystery novel *The Last Train* (and the forthcoming *Thai Girl in Tokyo* and *Japan Hand*) feature Detective Hiroshi Shimizu who investigates white collar crime in Tokyo. He writes regularly for many publications, including *The Japan Times*, *Newsweek Japan*, *Jazznin*, *Jazz Colo[u]rs*, and *Artscape Japan*; and runs his own website, *Jazz in Japan*. He is a professor of American Literature at Meiji Gakuin University where he teaches seminars in contemporary novels and film adaptations.

Becky Selengut is a cooking teacher, private chef, not-so-private comedian, and a prolific food writer. Her books include *The Washington Local and Seasonal Cookbook* (2008); *Good Fish: Sustainable Seafood Recipes from the Pacific Coast* (2011 and 2018); *Shroom: Mind-Bendingly Good Recipes for Cultivated and Wild Mushrooms* (2014); *Not One Shrine: Two Food Writers Devour Tokyo* (2016); and *How to Taste: The Curious Cook's Handbook to seasoning and balance, from umami to acid and beyond* (2018). In her spare time she co-hosts Look Inside *This Book Club*, a NSFW comedy podcast with Matthew Amster-Burton that discusses the free Kindle preview — and ONLY the preview — of bestselling books, usually while sipping Pinot Grigio.

Nisi Shawl is an African-American writer, editor, and journalist. She is best known as an author of fantasy and science fiction who writes and teaches about how fantastic fiction might reflect real-world diversity of gender, sexual orientation, race, colonialism, physical ability, age, and other sociocultural factors. Her debut novel, *Everfair*, was a 2016 Nebula Awards finalist, and her short stories have appeared in *Asimov's Science Fiction*, the *Infinite Matrix*, *Strange Horizons*, *Semiotext(e)* and numerous other magazines and anthologies. Her story collection Filter House was one of two winners of the 2008 James Tiptree, Jr. Award. During the ceremony, she was crowned with the Tiptree tiara and given a plaque, a check, a pie, and a ceramic sculpture of a duck.

You, Too, May Become a Taxidermist!

All of us at Regulus Press wish to extend our thanks and appreciation to everyone who participated in this year's Literary Taxidermy Short Story Competition. Your enthusiasm and commitment far exceeded our expectations — as did the *overwhelming* number of story submissions we received for each contest.

If you didn't participate this year and are coming to this collection of stories new to the idea of literary taxidermy, we hope you've enjoyed what you've found. And if you're a writer, we encourage you — the present reader — to become a future author.

Regulus Press plans to host another literary taxidermy competition, and we're looking for writers, both amateur and professional, to stitch together new and imaginative stories. The competition is your chance to get your hands dirty and join the growing community of literary taxidermists.

For the latest on the competition (and to learn more about the possibilities of literary taxidermy), visit:

www.literarytaxidermy.com

We all look forward to seeing what you come up with!

About the Editor

Mark Malamud is principal and manager of busymonster, LLC, a consultancy company focused on advanced user interface and design. His collection of short stories, *The Gymnasium*, established the idea of literary taxidermy. His novel, *Float the Pooch*, which pits David Bowie against Stanley Kubrick against a background of alien invasion, future sex, and Yom Kippur, is widely unread. He holds over 700 patents, and in 2012 he was the 8th most-prolific inventor of patents in the US. His current interests include breathing, the stroke of midnight, shaggy-dog wind-ups, and vowels.

Other Books from Regulus Press

One Thing Was Certain

An anthology of literary taxidermy based on the first and last lines of *Through the Looking-Glass* by Lewis Carroll. Award-winning stories from the 2018 Literary Taxidermy Short Story Competition.

Telephone Me Now

An anthology of literary taxidermy based on the first and last lines of "A Telephone Call" by Dorothy Parker. Award-winning stories from the 2018 Literary Taxidermy Short Story Competition.

The Gymnasium

Nineteen tales of melancholy and wonder created by "re-stuffing" what goes in-between the opening and closing lines of classic works by Milan Kundera, Philip K. Dick, Thomas Wolfe, Ian Fleming, and others. Short stories by Mark Malamud.

A Pocketful of Fish

An omnibus collection of poetry from North America's "most redoubtable poet." Includes the complete *Swimming through the Darkness* (1974), *Roe Roe Roe Your Boat* (1978), and *Will You Hold My Breath* (1994). Ichthyic poems by Choo 3T Fish.